More Best-Loved
Stories
Told at the
National Storytelling
Festival

More Best-Loved
Stories

Told at the
National Storytelling
Festival

Selected by the
National Association for the
Preservation and Perpetuation of Storytelling

THE NATIONAL STORYTELLING PRESS
Jonesborough, Tennessee

Distributed to the book trade by August House Publishers • P.O. Box 3223 • Little Rock, Ark. 72203

Published by the National Storytelling Press
of the National Association for the
Preservation and Perpetuation of Storytelling
P.O. Box 309 ■ Jonesborough, Tenn. 37659 ■ 800-525-4514

Printed in the United States

97 96 95 94 93   5 4 3 2 1

Project direction by Jimmy Neil Smith
Edited by Mary C. Weaver
Designed by Jane L. Hillhouse

Library of Congress Cataloging-in-Publication Data

More Best-Loved Stories Told at the National Storytelling Festival/selected
    by the National Association for the Preservation and Perpetuation of
    Storytelling—20th anniversary edition
        p. cm.
    Includes index.
    ISBN 1-879991-09-8 (hardcover); ISBN 1-879991-08-X (softcover)
    1. Tales. 2. Tales—United States. I. National Association for the
Preservation and Perpetuation of Storytelling (U.S.) II. Title.
    GR73.N38 1992   92-32631
    398.2—dc20   CIP

With gratitude to those
who tell—and especially to
those who listen.

Contents

PREFACE

This book represents an attempt—our second—to capture and preserve on paper the flavor of the National Storytelling Festival, the original and most prestigious event of its kind in the United States. For two decades the festival and the organization that shepherds it have grown and prospered, helping to catalyze the ongoing renaissance of storytelling in America.

Today storytelling takes place not just casually, on front porches, or formally, on stages, but everywhere in between. Professional tellers, yes, but also teachers, librarians, therapists, parents, and others are making storytelling and story-listening part of their work and life. They are the ones who day by day breathe life into the art of storytelling.

So as we mark 20 years of the National Storytelling Festival, we're really celebrating the people who've made it possible: the storytellers from around the world, representing every conceivable style and tradition, and the listeners—60 in 1973, the festival's first year; 6,000 in 1991. This year, who knows?

And of course, we're celebrating the hundreds of tales the festival tellers have shared with us. This collection presents 39 of the best: stories that exemplify the richness of this world's storytelling traditions yet reflect surprisingly universal themes.

Here you'll find stories from Japan, Zimbabwe, Norway, Israel, Vietnam, Persia, and Nova Scotia. You'll also discover a wealth of tales from cultures closer to home—stories whose origins are Native American, Appalachian, African-American, Western, and Southern.

In their deceptively simple manner, stories help us appreciate the diversity of other traditions while revealing the common threads that unite us. As storytellers relate their characters' individual sorrows, joys, and struggles, they also paint a picture of the human condition. And when we engage in open-hearted listening and telling, we experience the truth that what we hold in common runs far deeper than all that divides us.

The National Association for the Preservation and Perpetuation of Storytelling (NAPPS), the sponsor of the National Storytelling Festival, is a nonprofit organization dedicated to promoting the practice and application of storytelling. Founded in 1975, NAPPS now counts as members some 6,000 storytellers and story enthusiasts from all walks of life, living in every state of the union and two dozen foreign countries.

THE BOY WITH A KEG

Carol L. Birch

There once was a boy who was apprenticed to a man way up north in the mountains of Norway. The man was a master at brewing beer—beer so good that nothing else like it was to be found. When it came time for the boy to leave his apprenticeship, the master went to pay him, but the boy refused the money. He asked only for a keg of the richest Christmas brew. Well, that he got.

He went on his way, carrying the keg of beer for a long, long time. Now, you know if you've ever carried anything heavy, the longer you go, the heavier it gets. The boy began to look around to see if there was anyone with whom he could drink. With less beer in the keg, it would be lighter.

After a while he saw an old man with a great white beard.

"Good day," said the man.

"Good day to you," said the boy.

"Where are you going?" asked the man.

"Well, I'm looking for someone to drink with so I can make my keg lighter."

"Can't you drink with me?" asked the man. "I've traveled both far and wide, so I am tired and thirsty."

"I suppose I can," said the boy. "But tell me, what sort of man are you, and from where do you come?"

"I am God, and I come from heaven above."

"Well, I won't drink with you. You make some people rich, while others struggle in poverty. No, I won't drink with the likes of you." The boy took up his keg of beer, and off he trudged.

When he had gone a bit farther, the weight of the keg made him pause. And he knew he would have to sit by the road and wait until someone came by with whom he could drink to make the keg lighter.

At last an ugly, skinny man came rushing by.

"Good day," said the man.

After I took a trip through Norway, this story—which I'd been telling for years— took on new meaning. So many people I met there cared passionately about fairness and argued fiercely about religion. Their concerns are echoed in this story.

13

"Good day to you," said the boy.

"Where are you going?" asked the man.

"I'm waiting for someone to drink with so I can make my keg lighter."

"Can't you drink with me?" asked the man. "I've traveled both far and wide, so I am tired and thirsty."

"I suppose I can," said the boy. "But tell me, what sort of man are you, and from where do you come?"

"I am the devil, and I come from hell below."

"Well, I won't drink with you. You trouble and torment people, and whenever there is trouble, people always say it is your fault." So the boy took up his keg of beer, and off he trudged.

When he had gone only a little farther, he had to stop again by the side of the road to wait for someone to come by with whom he could drink. His keg was too heavy to carry.

After a while a man came by who was so old and withered that it was a wonder he hung together at all.

"Good day," wheezed the man.

"Good day to you," said the boy.

"Where are you going?" asked the man.

"I'm looking for someone to drink with so I can make my keg lighter. It's gotten too heavy to carry."

"Can't you drink with me?"

"I suppose I can. But tell me, what sort of man are you, and from where do you come?"

"They call me Death."

"Well, I will drink with you. You're a worthy man. You treat everyone the same, rich and poor."

So the boy and Death took turns drinking the beer, and the keg was soon lighter. At last Death said, "I've never known a drink that tasted better or did me so much good. I feel like a new man, and I want to give you a gift."

Death thought for a while and then said, "This keg will not weigh you down, and it will never be empty. And not only will the beer taste good, but it will be a healing drink so that you can make the sick well again. Whenever you enter the room of a sick person, you will see me—but you alone will see me. If I am at the foot of the bed, a sip of this drink will help the sick person recover at once. But if I am at the head of the bed—I want you to understand this—neither a sip of this beer nor any other medicine will help that person. I will have my way!"

The boy thanked Death for his gift, and they parted friends.

Soon everyone knew about the boy and his keg of beer. He was summoned from far and wide. He helped back to health people for whom there had been no hope. When he came into a sickroom, he saw where Death was sitting. He would offer the beer or not, and those who sipped it were saved. So you see, in this way the boy was always right. His fame grew, and so did his wealth.

One day the king of a neighboring country summoned the boy. The king's daughter was dangerously ill, and no doctor was able to save her. The king promised half his kingdom to the boy if he could save the princess. The boy entered the room and saw Death sitting at the head of the bed.

"This is a question of life and death," said the boy. "Indeed, nothing will save your daughter."

Frantic, the king said he would give the boy all of his kingdom if he cured the princess.

The boy looked squarely at Death. Death was dozing, so the boy motioned to the servants to turn the bed quickly and quietly, so that Death was now at the foot of the bed. The boy offered the princess a sip of the beer, and she recovered at once.

Death awoke to the cries of joy and said to the boy, "You've cheated me, and we are no longer friends!"

"I had to do it," said the boy. "He gave me all of his kingdom."

"That won't help you. You saved her, so now you're mine."

"What?" asked the boy. "I must die? Please let me say the Lord's Prayer before I die."

Death agreed. And knowing that Death could not go back on his word, the boy said many, many words, but he took care never to say the Lord's Prayer. "Our Father . . . " never passed his lips, and he thought he had Death cheated once and for all.

But Death realized the boy's deceit. One night he went into the boy's room and hung the Lord's Prayer on a board above the bed. When the boy awoke the next day, he began to read the words of the prayer. Before he realized it, he had read the final word: Amen.

Southbury, Connecticut, storyteller Carol L. Birch tells tales that leave people with memories worth having. A teacher, recording artist, and producer, she is writing a book on the aesthetics of storytelling. Her forthcoming audiotape, Careful What You Wish For *(Frostfire, 1993), focuses on the joys found and tears shed when wishes come true.*

THE THREE BROTHERS

Peninnah Schram

Once there was a man who lived a life filled with good deeds, charity, and justice. When this man was about to die, he called his three sons to him and said, "My children, the time of my death is near. I have lived a long life. What I hope and pray for you is that you will live in peace with one another. Just as I have never taken an oath in anger, so you too must follow this path. Quarreling can lead to oath-taking, so try never to quarrel. Love God, as your beloved mother and I have taught you. Live in this cottage as your home, and take care of my beautiful spice garden. Guard it from thieves in the night. I bless you, my sons, as Jacob blessed his sons."

With tears in their eyes the sons promised to follow their father's wishes, and the old man gave his blessing to each of his sons. After the father died, the sons faithfully remembered his words and stood watch in the garden, each one taking his turn.

One night, as the eldest brother was guarding the place, a stranger mysteriously appeared. "I am Elijah the Prophet," said the newcomer, "and I have come to reward you for following your father's wishes. But you may choose only one of three wishes: to become wealthy, to have great knowledge, or to marry a good wife."

Without a moment's hesitation, the eldest brother cried out, "I want to be rich. I want to have the most money in the world."

Elijah took a gold coin from his pocket and placed it in the eldest brother's hand. "This coin will bring you great wealth," said Elijah. When the brother looked to see what was in his palm, Elijah disappeared.

The next night, as the second brother was standing guard, Elijah suddenly appeared again and offered him the same gifts. "I want to know everything. I want to be the wisest man in the world," replied the second brother. "Through this book you will become a great scholar," said Elijah as he placed a book in the brother's open hands. As the

As a child I was intrigued by the prophet Elijah, the Master of Miracles in his chameleonlike disguises, offering choices, bringing hope, and rewarding hospitality. Scientists have only just discovered that hope is the key to overcoming adversity. But that is exactly why Elijah stories have been told for centuries, year-round, in the Jewish oral tradition.

second brother looked to see what was in his hands, Elijah disappeared.

Now, on the next night the youngest brother was in the garden when Elijah appeared and gave him the same three choices. The youngest brother smiled and said, "A good wife is better than riches." He nodded to Elijah, indicating that this was his choice.

Elijah smiled too and answered, "Come! We must take a short journey together to find this good wife." And Elijah and the youngest brother started on their search.

By evening they were tired and stopped at an inn. While the young man slept, Elijah, who could understand the language of all creatures, listened to the barnyard animals talking to one another. And what did he hear? The chickens and geese said, "Oh, this young man must have committed a terrible sin if he is to marry the innkeeper's daughter. She is so vain, and her parents are wicked people." Elijah did not like what he heard, and in the morning the two of them continued on their way.

The next night they stopped at another inn. Elijah listened to the animals talking, and again he heard how hardhearted and dishonest the innkeepers were. Once more Elijah was displeased by what he had heard, so in the morning he and the youngest son continued walking.

Late in the afternoon they were tired again, and when they came to a small inn, they decided to stay for the night. That night Elijah heard the animals talking with great excitement: "Have you heard? Have you heard? This young man who just arrived must be a righteous man if he is destined to marry our innkeeper's daughter, for she is not only beautiful but also wise and kind, just like her parents."

Early the next morning Elijah went to see the innkeeper in order to arrange a marriage between the youngest brother and the innkeeper's daughter. The innkeeper was pleased but said, "My daughter must give her consent as well. If she agrees, then they will marry." The daughter had seen the handsome young man when he arrived the night before.

She had noticed his manner as he spoke with Elijah, and she had fallen in love with him. So the young woman readily gave her consent, and a marriage was arranged. Elijah performed the ceremony and then disappeared.

Soon afterward the couple returned to the young man's home. When they arrived at the cottage, they found that the two brothers had left: The eldest one had bought a mansion and moved there. The second brother was traveling around the world giving lectures, and wherever he went, he was acclaimed a great scholar and wise man. So the young couple planted the garden, sold the spices and herbs they raised in order to earn a living, had children, and lived together peacefully in their small home.

Several years passed, and Elijah decided to find out what had happened to the three brothers since he had visited them in the garden. Master of disguises that he was, Elijah assumed the appearance of a beggar and went to the rich brother's mansion. The servants refused to allow him in.

When the beggar called out, "I am here to reclaim what I have given your master," the eldest brother recognized the voice of Elijah. He came running to the door and pleaded with Elijah to allow him to keep the coin.

"No," said Elijah. "Give me back the coin I gave you. You have not used your wealth to help people in need. Instead you have become greedy and have used it for yourself alone. You are not worthy to keep the coin." And the eldest brother had to return the gold coin to Elijah.

Then, in the guise of a scholar, Elijah went to a discourse given by the second brother. He listened and then asked a question on a point of the law. The second brother ignored the question. But when Elijah asked it again, the brother rebuked him and said, "I have no time for such foolish questions."

"No time for answering even a foolish question?" asked Elijah. "What good then is your scholarship if you cannot take the time to teach and explain the complex ideas you are talking about? It might be better if you returned the book I gave you years ago, since all that you know comes from the book and not from your own questioning and learning."

The scholar immediately understood that this was Elijah, and he pleaded with him for another chance. But Elijah asked for the book. "You are not worthy to keep it," he said. And the second brother had to return the book.

Finally Elijah assumed the guise of a poor man and went to the home of the youngest brother. As he approached the house, the wife opened the door. Seeing a person who was tired and thirsty, she invited him in to rest, and she put food and drink on the table for him.

When he had rested, Elijah said to the couple, "I give you wealth and learning because of this good wife's deeds." And as Elijah handed them the gold coin and the book, he added, "In your home you will know how to use the wealth wisely and to help others, and you will know how to share your knowledge and learning for good and not for evil." Then Elijah blessed the couple and disappeared.

The couple lived a happy life for the rest of their days. And when they grew old, they gave the coin and the book to their children.

A professional storyteller since 1970, Peninnah Schram is an associate professor of speech and drama at Stern College of Yeshiva University in New York City. She is the author of three folk-tale collections, most recently Tales of Elijah the Prophet *(Jason Aronson, 1991). Schram is the founding director of the Jewish Storytelling Center at New York City's 92nd Street Y.*

THE CALICO COFFIN

Lee Pennington

A long time ago there was a beautiful girl with long, willowy hair that looked like sunlight on ripened grain. Her skin was as white as the underside of a dove. Her cheeks always had a red flush, but she used nothing for color—except now and then when she pinched her cheeks just a little before going to a square dance.

One day in May the young girl took ill. Her skin lost its glow and turned gray, and the rosy red color left her cheeks. Her mother nursed her—gathered herbs, boiled tea, and gave the drink to her daughter. But the girl became sicker and sicker, and by morning, when the pale sun slipped over the green hilltop and the lifting fog, she was dead. Her spirit left her quietly while her mother slept.

When the mother arose, the girl lay still under the bright many-colored quilt. The mother rubbed her eyes to chase away the sleep, to try to see her daughter's breathing, but the bed was quiet. She touched her daughter, but there was a chill as cold and gray and damp as the stillness of the room. She walked to the window and stood there, watching the sun rise and the fog spin off in little patterns. Then her tears came, and she could no longer see the sun or the fog.

Later in the day the girl's father and brother waded through sedge grass, carrying mattocks and shovels. Near a little brownish-green cedar tree and seven vertical stones—all homemade and with names and dates chiseled into them—they dug the grave.

When they returned to the house, the mother, her eyes pained with grief, was standing on the porch.

"We can bury her in the cedar box—the one made for me," she said. "I can wait." Then she turned and went into the house.

The father and son went to the barn, and in the loft they found the cedar coffin—long and narrow, completely lined in cotton calico, top to bottom. Together they lowered the box to the ground and carried it, the father in front, the son behind, to the house.

When I was growing up in the Southern Appalachian Mountains, I heard this tale told as a true story. In that time and place, stories were the bloodline, and people were the heart. I wonder now how we could've survived without the yarns that entertained us, made us laugh and cry, and enriched our lives.

"She's ready," said the mother. The young girl lay silently upon the bed, dressed in a white gown. "She's wearing my wedding dress. She's just the size I was then."

They placed her body in the calico coffin, carried it to the cemetery, and lowered it into the ground. By the time the sun had pulled every trace of light from the hill, the father threw the last shovelful of fresh dirt upon the mound, and they returned home.

The son was exhausted, so he climbed the stairs to his bedroom and quickly fell asleep. But long before morning he was awakened by a horrible scream. He sat up in bed and stared around the upstairs room and then out the window, but there was no moon, and he could see nothing.

He heard another scream, full and shattering, coming from downstairs. So he quickly dressed, hurried down the stairway into his parents' bedroom, and found his father trying to comfort his mother.

The mother screamed again, and the young boy felt chills shudder through his body.

"I know she's alive!" she wailed. "I know she's alive! I hear her calling! You must go to her!"

The father looked at his son, standing by his mother's bed with his eyes full of fright. The two stayed with her throughout the night, but when morning came, she was still screaming, pleading, begging.

"Please! You've got to dig her up! She's alive! I hear her calling!" The father turned to his son and whispered, "We have to do it. We must show her, prove to her that your sister's dead, or she'll never recover from this agony."

So the three of them slipped into the morning to the graveyard, and the father and son dug open the grave as the mother stood over them, watching and weeping. The wind swept through her long, graying hair, making shadows on the freshly turned earth.

Finally the shovels touched the box. The father and son worked ropes under it and eased it up and out of the grave. With the point of the shovel, the father pried open the coffin lid—the lid he had nailed down only the day before.

The father looked at the mother, then the son, and slowly lifted the lid. Then, horror-stricken, the father dropped his shovel and fell back. The mother sank down onto the ground, and her tears came even heavier. The son fell upon his knees in the fresh dirt.

The young girl lay in the calico coffin. Her white dress was torn at the neck, and her face, no longer beautiful, was contorted and twisted in pain. Her fingernails were gone, and her fingers and hands were covered with blood. The coffin's calico lining was shredded to bits, and underneath the lid were fingernail marks deeply carved into the wood.

Lee Pennington grew up in Eastern Kentucky in a family of storytellers. A poet, writer, folk singer, and storyteller, Pennington has taught English and creative writing since 1967 at Jefferson Community College in Louisville, Kentucky. In 1984 he was named his state's poet laureate.

THE RED THREAD

Martha Holloway

This is my adaptation of a story from Persian Folk and Fairy Tales Retold by Anne Sinclair Mehdevi *(Chatto & Windus, 1966). Enchanted by its symbolism, a couple chose it for me to tell at their wedding—and enlisted one of their grandmothers to play the part of the old woman sewing with a red thread.*

There was a time, and there was not a time in the long ago, when there lived in Persia a young man whose name was Bahram. He was the son of a cocoon peeler who made his living by unwinding the silk thread from the cocoons of the silkworms that feed on mulberry leaves.

The father died, leaving his widow and son very poor. And the son, trying to carry on his father's trade, took the family's remaining 100 dirhams, the last bit of money they had, and went to the bazaar to buy some cocoons to peel. There he came upon three men beating a bag with a stick. Loud yowls and cries were coming from inside the bag, and Bahram asked what was inside it.

"We have a cat in here," they answered.

"Why do you beat the poor animal?" said Bahram. "Open the bag, and let it go."

They laughed and said, "If your heart burns so for this cat, give us 100 dirhams, and the cat will be yours."

So Bahram gave them his last 100 dirhams and set the cat free. She looked up at him, rubbed against his leg, and said, "Kindness is never forgotten. Here is a magic ring. Rub it, and the slave of the ring will give you anything—from the milk of a hen to the mountains of the moon. But take care that it does not fall into the hands of an unworthy person."

Bahram took the ring home to the little mud hut where he lived with his mother, told her about the powers of the ring, and said to her, "From this day our bread is buttered, and our tongues shall taste nothing but raspberry juice."

"What will you do first?" asked his mother.

"First I'm going to destroy this little mud hut and wish for a castle."

"No, my son," she said. "Leave this hut, which your father built with his own hands and in which you were born. It is filled with sweet memories for me. Wish for a castle for yourself next door, but leave the

24

hut. I will live here, and you can live in the castle."

Bahram agreed and rubbed the ring. Instantly he had everything he desired: the castle, expensive clothes, fine food, and beautiful horses. The only thing he lacked was a wife.

One day not long afterward he was riding past the king's palace. On the balcony he saw the king's daughter, combing her hair. She was as beautiful as the moon in its 14th night, and he thought, *This is the girl who must be my wife.*

He went home and told his mother to go to the palace and ask for the hand of the princess. This she did, dressed simply, in her cotton dress and cotton shoes, like a poor woman.

The king said to her, "Do you think I would give my daughter to the son of a poor woman? Anyone who wants to marry my daughter must give me seven camels loaded with silver, put seven diamond buttons in my daughter's crown, provide seven barrels of pure gold, and bring seven rugs woven with pearls to put beneath my daughter's feet. If you cannot do these things, you shall be slain for your impertinence."

The woman said, "Say 70 instead of seven, and it will be done."

The king replied, "Bring what I ask, and take what you want." The mother went home and told Bahram what the king had said, and at once the dowry was furnished.

In this way Bahram won the hand of the princess, and they were married. A seven-day feast was held. But in the excitement of the celebration the couple forgot one thing: the red thread. For it is written that at every wedding there must be present an old woman sewing with a red thread, which will forever sew together the lips of those people with evil tongues who might bring disaster to the marriage with their smooth, lying words.

Bahram was happy, the princess was happy, and Bahram's mother was happy in her little mud hut next door to the castle. But far away in the land of the Tatars, the prince of Tatary was not happy. He had loved the king's daughter for many a year, and he had sent his messengers to ask for her hand. When they returned and told him that she had married a cocoon peeler's son, he flew into a rage. "How could a cocoon peeler's son marry a princess? How could he furnish such a rich dowry?"

He said to himself, "I shall take the princess from the cocoon peeler's son. I shall discover his secret."

Now, there lived in Tatary a wicked old woman who was famous for her smooth, lying tongue. The prince of Tatary sent for her and said, "Go to the town where the cocoon peeler's son lives. Find out where he gets his wealth and how I can get the princess. Do this, and I will give you silver equal to your weight."

The old woman rode on a donkey till she came to the town where Bahram dwelt in his castle with his wife. She was hired as a servant in the castle and soon became a favorite of the princess, for she amused her by telling many stories.

One day the old woman said, "Although your father is a king, he is poorer than your husband, who is only a cocoon peeler's son. Have you never wondered how your husband got all his wealth?"

"No, I never wondered," the princess answered.

"You ought to ask him," the old woman said. "It will be of use to you someday to know how your husband became so rich."

That night the princess said, "Dear husband, though you are only a cocoon peeler's son, you are wealthier than my father. How did you get your riches?"

Bahram became angry and told her not to ask about things that did not concern her. The princess was hurt by his rough words. Her heart tightened, and she grew sad and wept. Then Bahram relented and said, "My wealth comes from a magic ring that was given me for a kindness I did long ago."

"Where is this ring?"

"It is hidden in the rafters of the ceiling. But this is a secret you must not tell, for if an unworthy person gets the ring, the lord of evil will enter his heart and turn the world upside-down."

The princess promised to keep the secret, but the next day when the old woman again asked her about her husband's riches, she forgot her promise, telling her servant about the ring and where it was hidden. A few days later the old woman found a chance to steal the ring, and she took it back to the prince of Tatary.

When he rubbed the ring, the slave of the ring appeared. The prince said, "I wish to have the princess for my wife, and I wish for the cocoon peeler's son to lose everything he has."

In a twinkling it was done. Bahram's castle vanished. Nothing remained but the little mud hut of his mother. And the princess found herself standing before the prince of Tatary. She wept and refused to utter a word.

Bahram was riding in the desert with a few servants, when he suddenly found himself on the ground, the horse and servants gone and his fine clothes turned into the cotton doublet and trousers he had been wearing the day he saved the cat. He walked home to the hut of his mother, and she told him how all had disappeared between one blink of her eyes and the next. Bahram was ready to die of grief over the loss of his wife, but his mother said, "What the wind gives, the wind takes away. I have saved a few dirhams. Take them, buy some cocoons, and start in business as your father did."

So the next day, with bowed head and broken heart, Bahram went to town to inquire from door to door whether anyone had cocoons to sell. He found none. Toward sunset he was tired and sat down to rest, his head on his knees. As he sat there, the cat he had saved came to him and asked why he was crouched thus on the knees of sorrow.

"Someone with an unclean heart has taken the ring from me," he said, "and he has also taken my beloved wife, my castle, and all my possessions, leaving me with nothing to eat but the salt of my tears."

The cat said, "I will help you once more, for a kindness is never forgotten."

Then the cat asked all the other animals, "Who knows where Bahram's wife has gone? Who knows the name of his enemy?"

The sparrow said, "It is the old woman with the smooth tongue who ate her way into the heart of the princess. She stole the ring. I saw it all from my perch near the window. This old woman is the servant of the prince of Tatary."

So the cat made her way to the palace of Tatary, crept in, and found the princess weeping. "Do not weep, O princess. I have been sent by your husband to save you, if you will only tell me where the prince of Tatary keeps the ring."

"Alas," said the princess. "He always keeps it on his finger except when he sleeps. Then he puts it in his mouth so no one can take it."

The next evening when the prince had gone to sleep, the cat slipped into the kitchen of the palace and sat down in front of a mouse hole. When the mouse came out, she pounced on him and said, "Look, brother, I can crush you between my teeth as easily as drink water. If you want to stay alive, you must do as I say."

"Speak, and I shall obey," said the mouse.

The cat said, "Dip your tail into the pepper pot, and come with me." The mouse did so and followed the cat to the bedroom of the prince, who was sound asleep.

"Do as I command you," said the cat.

"I obey," said the mouse. After the cat had instructed him, he ran softly across the prince's chest and stuck his peppery tail up the prince's nose. The prince sneezed, and the ring flew out of his mouth. The cat caught it and hurried back to Bahram, who rubbed the ring, and once again all was as it had been before.

When Bahram had embraced his wife, he asked her who had tricked her, and she told him about the old woman. "You should not have been deceived by a smooth, lying tongue," he said, "but it was not your fault, for at our wedding we forgot the red thread."

Then the two were married again, and this time they made sure to have at the ceremony an old woman sewing with red thread—the thread that sews together the lips of people with smooth, lying tongues who might bring disaster to the marriage.

As for the ring, in order to keep it from falling into the hands of an unworthy person, Bahram threw it into the depths of the ocean, where it remains to this day.

Bahram and the princess lived long in joy and happiness. From that day their bread was always buttered, and their tongues tasted nothing but raspberry juice.

Native Texan Martha Holloway believes stories should be told to share both joy and wisdom. Concerned about what she sees as the growing commercialism of storytelling, she cautions that when the clear glass of the story is covered with a veneer of silver, it becomes a mirror in which the teller sees not truth but self. Holloway lives in La Jolla, California.

CHESTER BEHNKE GOES HUNTING

John Basinger

Over time I've grown close to my character Chester Behnke. I named him for a deceased relative—it's a way of staying in touch. Although Chester has related four stories to me so far, he complains that I don't listen to him enough. I know that I'll be hearing from him when he sees his story in print.

Before I tell you this story, there are a few things you have to know about Chester Behnke: He was born in Chicago of indeterminate parentage, so any family he has, he has picked up along the way. The other thing is that if you had to choose one word to describe him, that word would probably be *incomplete*. Now on with the story.

Heppner's Point wasn't more than two miles away, but 13-year-old Chester Behnke was preparing for his hunting trip there as if his subscription to *Field and Stream* depended on it. And in a way it did, because Chester planned to write up his expedition and send it to them. That seemed right because it was *Field and Stream* that had given him the idea of a hunting trip in the first place.

The magazine's stories transported him to exotic places—like the upper reaches of the Amazon rain forest to hunt jaguars or to Kodiak Island to track the enormous kodiak bear. Well, there weren't any bears or jaguars to speak of on the farms around Mountain Lake, a small town in the rolling hills of southwestern Minnesota, but Chester had noticed a lot of small mammals, many of which were surely wild enough.

So he got out of bed that cold gray Saturday morning in October and pulled on his trousers, shirt, sweater, windbreaker, and hunting boots. He had been soaking the latter in neat's-foot oil for the past three months, so if the house were ever buried by an especially bad dust storm blowing up from the plains, those boots would still be supple 3,000 years later when archaeologists dug up the town.

Chester ran downstairs to eat breakfast. When Aunt Marie asked him why the get-up, he explained he was going hunting right after breakfast. "Right after you've done the chores," Aunt Marie corrected. That wasn't part of the plan at all, but Aunt Marie wouldn't be swayed, so Chester soon found himself on all fours, dusting the dining-room furniture. For sure he wouldn't write about this part of the day for *Field and Stream*.

After he had swept the front and back sidewalks down to the street and ridden his bike downtown for the groceries, he ran to the attic to get his single-shot Winchester .22 and a handful of shells—shorts. Longs had more killing power, but they carried about a mile, and in the unlikely event of his missing his prey, he didn't want to accidentally bag someone in town. He dug out his Boy Scout gear from the closet, strapped on his big black war-surplus Marine K-Bar knife, stopped in the kitchen long enough to pack a bread-and-jelly sandwich—just in case—and he was off.

He ran down the back steps, along the back sidewalk (nice and clean now), past the trees bursting with apples—he grabbed one— across the street, through the schoolyard, and up the block past the house his seventh-grade teacher, Rachel Boxrud, roomed in. Then he turned left down the street that ran past B.J.'s house.

Chester hoped that B.J. would be coming out just as he passed; he even slowed down, but no luck. He glanced at the spot on her front lawn, the little strip of grass between the sidewalk and the curb, where he'd wrestled T.C. for her affections the past summer. The recollection still caused him pain. Chester was executing a pinning move—victory and B.J. were his as he swung his right leg over his rival—and farted. Loudly! The fight ended with T.C.'s bellowing "I win," followed by a lot of giggling and an embarrassed leave-taking, and that was that. Chester never recovered the lost ground. B.J. later married T.C., who became an All-American in track and came within a hamstring-pull of making the Olympic team. If T.C. ever farted, it was surely not in B.J.'s hearing.

At the end of B.J.'s block Chester turned right and headed north. If he kept going straight, he could take the shortcut to Heppner's Point. But that led through a big slough, and there were serious rumors of quicksand there. Now, that was just the story for *Field and Stream*, but not if he didn't make it back to tell the tale! Saving that adventure for another time, he took the long way around.

The road he was on was officially known as Third Avenue, but since there were no street signs in town yet, the kids named the streets according to who lived on them or where they led. This one was accordingly called the lake road or the cemetery road, depending on your destination. There had once been a lake southeast of town, but that had long since been drained by the Russian Mennonite immigrants for the rich bottom land, leaving stranded in the mud an 84-and-a-half-foot-high mound that served as the settlement's mountain. As a mountain it was undoubtedly the world's lowest, but as the old-timers said, it was snowcapped every winter. As for the lake, well, in the 1930s the town fathers (including Chester's Uncle Harvey) got up a WPA project and had a creek north of town dammed up. The resulting backed-up water produced an artificial lake that wasn't very big, but it did restore some credibility to the town's name.

The lake road took Chester past his cousin Sheetzy's house, behind which some people kept up a clay tennis court, the only one in town except for the one behind the school. That one got swallowed up years later when the school expanded. Now the school building is twice as big as it was and has half the students. Worse yet, to pull together an 11-man football team, Mountain Lake had to consolidate—just for the football season—with Butterfield, a little grease spot half the size of Mountain Lake (population 1,760) and six miles away. But since Butterfield had already consolidated with Odin, the result of all this consolidation is the dreadful double hyphenation Mountain Lake-Butterfield-Odin.

About a mile past Sheetzy's the road ran up a hill, and there at the top, overlooking the lake and Heppner's Point, were the Gospel Mennonite Church on the right and the cemetery on the left. The preacher at the church was the Reverend John P. Ruderman, who was forever coming from Hopiland with news of fresh conversions and going back to Hopiland with the money taken in the collection to garner more. Reverend Ruderman would teach the release-time religious-education class that Chester would take in his junior year of high school. The reverend would spend the entire year showing how the book of Revelation conclusively proved that the Roman Catholic Church was the infamous Whore of Babylon. (There was a lot of interest in the Whore of Babylon in Mountain Lake during those pre–Vatican Council years.)

As for the cemetery, Chester knew that his aunt and uncle planned to be buried there, but he didn't. There might be a memorial stone there, but he was pretty sure his remains would be moldering in an unmarked grave somewhere along the Amazon or frozen in the permafrost up in the tundra. Such was the real adventurer's fate, he'd read.

At the top of the hill the blacktop ran out, and the road turned to gravel. Partway down the other side Chester saw the very rock that had been his undoing that summer. He had been racing bikes with T.C., comfortably in the lead, when his wobbly front wheel hit the rock. After a series of sickening side-to-side lurches—like in *The Bad and the Beautiful*, when Lana Turner was in that car in the dark, careering down the highway, completely out of control—the bike jackknifed, and he flew over the handlebars and skidded on his face. T.C. shot by, went all the way to the bottom, then turned back up and loudly claimed victory. Chester's bike got a broken frame from the force of the bouncing, and he had a swollen face and a few scars that lasted five years before they faded away.

At the bottom of the hill was the little beach where Red Cross swimming instruction was held every summer. Novice swimmers began with their age group and metamorphosed from tadpoles to minnows to jellyfish or whatever, paddling their way up the evolutionary ladder of swimming skill to sharks or whales. Since Chester worked all summer on a farm, he never got any instruction; so he taught himself, a habit he'd formed a few years before when he was living in Chicago and went to the North Avenue YMCA. He'd hold onto the pool gutter with one hand, stroke with the other, kick his feet, and then switch hands at the other end. After a while he'd put it all together and sink, thrashing, to the bottom.

Most of the time the big kids would go over to the dam and dive off the three-foot-high pillars to the water below, which was all of nine feet deep. The dam was also where the best fishing was, which added the worry of possibly diving too deep and getting entangled in old fishing lines and maybe being trapped down there in the cool mud and coffee-colored water, or at least having an eye put out with a rusty fishhook. One summer one of old Joe Hilderbrandt's boys took the hood off Joe's maroon '41 Ford, turned it over, and used it as a boat. Not having metamorphosed up the evolutionary swimming ladder, the boy couldn't swim, so when the little craft took on water and sank, he did too. A younger brother who'd accompanied him survived and went on to become the owner of three banks in the hyphenated towns.

Following along the road as it swung below the cemetery, Chester finally arrived at Heppner's Point. He climbed through a barbed-wire fence, tearing his trousers a little bit; cut across the pasture, on the lookout for the big bull old man Heppner kept there; and came to the grove of oak trees. Now stealth was in order, for Chester planned to shoot some squirrels and take them along to the Second Island, where he'd build a fire and cook them.

He looked around, and sure enough, there stood a big fat red squirrel. Chester tested the wind, checked for cover, dropped down on his belly, and began stalking it just the way he'd read about in *Field and Stream.* The squirrel was out a little ways between two trees, gathering acorns. Chester pulled a shell out of his pocket, loaded the rifle, centered the little gold bead at the end of the barrel square on the head of the squirrel, and proceeded with his BRASS steps (breathe, release, aim, slack, squeeze).

Nothing happened. What a boneheaded mistake! He'd forgotten to release the safety! Chester had a little trouble with that word. That's what the older kids called rubbers, and that sort of thing made him nervous, especially one time in school, when the buxom Miss Boxrud had asked him if he wanted to be on the Safety Patrol. He turned beet red right in front of her. When she divined the direction of his thoughts, she blushed too.

Chester tried it again. Holding the rifle with his right arm, he closed his right eye, sighted along the barrel with his left, centered the gold bead right on the squirrel's head, squeezed off a round just as *Field and Stream* had instructed, and missed. He loaded up again, went through the same business with the eyes, did his BRASS extra carefully this time, and missed again. And again. And again! The squirrel, unfazed by the popping sounds, went on sniffing for acorns.

What was wrong? Chester had to hit the thing. That was the whole reason for bringing along his deadly Marine K-Bar knife: to skin the squirrel. One time he and his brother Allen had had a standoff in the back yard, his brother with a bow and arrow and he with his K-Bar. Chester warned him, but Allen shot anyhow. So after the little blunt arrow bounced off his chest, Chester kind of tossed the knife underhand at his brother and hit him in the knee. Oh my, did Chester get it that night. His protestation that Allen had shot first didn't wash.

"That was just a toy. Your knife could have killed him!" screamed Aunt Marie. Well, Chester allowed that the K-Bar was a real weapon, but number one, it was dull; number two, he hadn't thrown it hard; and number three, he'd never heard of anyone dying from a stab wound to the kneecap.

Bang! Chester shot and missed again. In frustration he picked up a clump of dirt and threw it at the squirrel. This got the squirrel's attention, and it ran for a tree. Chester followed, snapping off rounds as he ran. The squirrel led him three or four times around the tree before skittering out on a limb high enough up that Chester couldn't get a good angle on the shot. He fired and missed again.

Chester didn't realize the problem. You see, he was right-handed, but his right eye was severely astigmatic, so he naturally favored his good left one. Of course, sighting along the barrel with this left eye pulled the barrel off to the left of a true aim, so he would have to have been right on top of the squirrel to hit it. But *parallax* was a word he wouldn't hear until the Army got him and switched him over to shooting left-handed. Thereupon he discovered he was a natural shot. All he had to do was visualize T.C.'s rear end in the bull's eye, and he qualified as expert with every weapon the Army possessed. Meanwhile, he missed and missed again. Now he would never see the write-up in *Field and Stream*: How I Faced Down a Rabid Squirrel That Rose Up on Its Hind Legs to Its Full Height and Charged Me!

Chester figured he'd have better luck with a kodiak bear, its being a bigger target. He was down to his last round and decided to save it. That was gospel. *Field and Stream* taught that a man shouldn't have a weapon without ammunition for it. Suppose Heppner's bull came at him as he crossed the pasture? Of course, a .22 short wasn't going to stop a bull unless Chester hit him in the eye, but since a bull's eye was about the same size as a squirrel's head, Chester knew what his chances were there.

It was time to get out of this pasture, trek on over to the Second Island, and institute Plan B: fishing. His Boy Scout kit contained a fishing line and hook. He got out his bread-and-jelly sandwich, broke off some of the Wonder Bread, rolled it into a ball, baited the hook, and looked for a place to throw in the line. If he'd been at the dam, he could have stood on the road and just dropped the line over the metal railing. But here the water was too shallow, and he had no pole. And on the whole island there was only one bush, the longest branch of which was no more than four feet. It would have to do. Chester got out his K-Bar, hacked away at the branch, stripped off the twigs, tied on the line, stepped onto a rock a few feet out in the lake, and fished.

The only fish in the lake were bullheads, along with some crappies and a few perch. That was it. Oh, there were rumors of trout, bass, and northern pike, but he'd never seen any. And the bullheads were mostly small, just big enough for you to step on over at the beach and puncture your foot with their spines. Nonetheless, he hoped for an epic fight with a 20-pound lunker that he'd finally land, muscles sore but face glowing. *Lunker* was a *Field and Stream* word meaning "a big trophy-sized granddaddy fish." But the few nibbles he got didn't seem promising.

Suddenly Chester got a bite, a strike—he felt it. He jerked up the branch, and there dangling at the end of the line was the usual Mountain Lake bullhead, all five inches of him. Chester didn't like bullheads, but intrepid explorers had to make do with what the land offered them. So he took the ugly thing, which looked like a stunted catfish. It didn't fight much. In fact, it didn't fight at all. It just hung on the hook and wiggled a little. Chester hoped it hadn't swallowed the hook. See, if the fish just hooked himself on the lip, Chester could work the hook off pretty quick and throw it back in or put it on a stringer, which he didn't have. But if the fish swallowed the hook, there was trouble because there was no way of getting it out without literally tearing the little guy's guts out. Chester turned squeamish at the thought. Yikes!

Sure enough, the fish had swallowed the hook. A fatal attraction for bread and jelly. What to do? Pull it out, Chester. You started this; now finish it! But that would hurt the thing, and it might start flopping around. Chester couldn't see what to do. He couldn't just leave the hook in; that was irresponsible. He could chop the fish's head off with the K-Bar, but the knife was so dull, he could foresee a sawing operation with all kinds of ugly possibilities. If the fish just weren't hooked like that, he'd throw it back. But here it was. Chester had done it, it was his responsibility, and he'd have to face it. *Field and Stream* would agree.

Then inspiration born of desperation hit him. Chester put the fish down on its yellow-gray belly, reached into his pocket, took out his last bullet (thank God he'd had the foresight to save one), and loaded the rifle. He put the barrel one inch away from the little guy's head, aimed (parallax and all), and fired.

There. He'd made his kill. A hunter has to make his kill. Now the day could go on. Chester built a little fire in the approved Boy Scout way, put his pan on it to heat, and set about cleaning the fish. Mercifully, bullheads have no scales, but they have about two billion bones. When he'd finished filleting the fish with the world's dullest deadly knife, he had two strips of flesh about the size of two sticks of Wrigley's Spearmint chewing gum. Dropping them into the pan, he squatted down to watch them fry. It sure wasn't much to look at, but it was real. It was as real as anything the famous explorers had ever done. He turned the fish with the K-Bar, and when it was done, about two minutes later, he scraped it out onto the face of his bread-and-jelly sandwich and ate it. Gingerly. The bones precluded any show of gusto, but who was there to see?

After he finished, he relaxed by the fire and thought over the day's adventures. Maybe he hadn't made it up to the Aleutian Islands, but he was definitely doing more than the rest of the kids in town were doing today. If only B.J. were here. He'd have given her some fish. Maybe the lunker would have struck for her.

Face it, Chester, face it. You'd rather be playing canasta at her house. Still, wasn't unrequited love behind most of the solitary, brave men of the world who went out adventuring? That part of it didn't get much play in *Field and Stream*, but Chester was sure it was true. So he hunkered down, burped a small burp, and through the wisps of smoke, stared east across the lake at his future—with or without B.J.

And that's where we'll leave Chester Behnke for now.

John Basinger is a long-time member of the National Theater of the Deaf and for 20 years taught theater and sign language at Mohegan Community College in Norwich, Connecticut. He writes stories, poetry, and plays and is actively engaged in helping other tellers stage their stories.

THE LEGEND OF OBI GUI GUI

Luisah Teish

This Yoruba tale from southwest Nigeria teaches humility and respect for kinship while showing the consequences of misplaced vanity. It also explains why coconuts fall from trees.

Let me ask you something: How many of you like coconut candy? Coconut cookies? Cake with coconut icing? Coconut-flavored ice cream? And coconut cream pie? If you like coconut, I want you to meet a friend of mine. His name is Obi Gui Gui, and that means "dried coconut."

Obi Gui Gui was the favorite son of the sun that shines up in the heavens, you see. Obi Gui Gui used to live way, way up in the tops of the trees, with plenty of sunshine and fresh air and beautiful leaves for curtains. His life was really good.

But on his 16th birthday something very strange happened to him. Obi Gui Gui called Elegba the messenger and said, "Elegba, darling, I'm having a birthday party, and I want you to invite the mayor, the banker, and the movie star."

Elegba said, "But, Obi Gui Gui, what about your aunt and uncle?" Obi Gui Gui said, "No. They can't come."

"What about your neighbors and friends?"

"Uh-uh. They ain't invited."

"What about the girls and boys you went to school with?"

Obi Gui Gui said, "No. They're too raggedy to come to my party."

When Elegba realized what was going on, he decided to play a trick on Obi Gui Gui. You know what he did? He walked through the rich part of town, and he said, "Party at Obi Gui Gui's at seven o'clock. Party at Obi Gui Gui's at seven o'clock." Then he went to the poor part of town, and he said, "Party at Obi Gui Gui's at nine o'clock. Party at Obi Gui Gui's at nine o'clock."

Then he ran all the way up to the sun and knocked on the door of Obi Gui Gui's daddy. When Olofi came to the door, he said, "Elegba, my friend, how wonderful to see you."

Elegba said, "You ain't going to be so happy to see me, Olofi. I come bringing bad news."

"But how can there be bad news on a beautiful day like today, when I am shining so brightly?"

"It's about your boy, Obi Gui Gui. He's got a bad case of the big-head. He's having a birthday party. He's inviting the rich and famous, and he's neglecting his own relatives, neighbors, and friends."

Olofi said, "Oh no, Elegba, don't come in here lying about my child! I taught my boy better than that."

Elegba said, "You think I'm lying? You weren't invited, were you?"

Olofi realized that he hadn't been invited, and he was Obi Gui Gui's daddy. So Olofi decided that he too would play a trick on Obi Gui Gui.

At six-thirty Obi Gui Gui put on his finest vines. He put the food on the table and the music on the box. At seven o'clock there was a knock on the door. "What's happening, y'all?" There were the mayor, the banker, and the movie star, and they partied, partied, partied.

At nine o'clock there came another knock. There at the door stood his aunt, his uncle, his neighbors, and his friends in raggedy clothes, with presents in their hands.

"No, you ain't coming to my party!"

"But, Obi Gui Gui, I am your uncle; this is your aunt. We changed your diapers when you were a baby. These are your neighbors and your friends and the girls and boys you went to school with. Can't we please come to your party?"

Obi Gui Gui shouted "No!" and slammed the door in their faces. They couldn't understand why he treated them like that. They'd always been good to him.

At nine-thirty the sun went down, and an old man in a dark cape knocked on Obi Gui Gui's door. "Is this the home of Obi Gui Gui?"

"Yes, old man, what do you want?"

"Is there a party here tonight? Can I come in?"

"There is a party, but your raggedy butt can't come in!"

"Do you know who I am? Are you sure you want to talk to me like that?"

"Look, old man, I don't care who you are. You ain't invited to this party. I'm going to stand in the doorway and watch you walk away, and if you ain't gone in three minutes, I am going to kick you out of the neighborhood."

"Okay, if that's the way you want it."

Obi Gui Gui stood in the doorway and watched as the old man started to walk away. Suddenly the stranger turned around and said, "Obi Gui Gui, look at who I really am!" And when he threw back his cape, the sun shone so brightly in Obi Gui Gui's face that he realized it was his daddy. He said, "Oh, Daddy"—sob, sob. "Don't beat my butt, Daddy. I didn't know it was you, Daddy . . . I mean, I knew it was you, and I was just playing. I mean, I thought it might have been you, Daddy"—sob, sob.

Olofi said, "I see that Elegba was right. You do have a bad case of the big-head. Now, what would be proper punishment for a young man like you?"

Olofi thought about it, and finally he said, "Obi Gui Gui, from now on you'll live way up in the tops of the trees, with plenty of sunshine and fresh air and beautiful leaves for curtains, and your life will be good. But the minute you get the big-head, your head will fall to the ground. People will roll it round and round, then smash it open and eat your insides out!"

So the next time you eat some coconut candy, coconut cookies, cake with coconut icing, coconut-flavored ice cream, or coconut cream pie, I want you to hold that coconut in front of you and say, "Obi Gui Gui, look at who I really am"—then eat him up. Because that's what he gets for having the big-head.

Luisah Teish of Oakland, California, is a writer, storyteller, and ritualist. The author of Jambalaya: The Natural Woman's Book of Personal Charms and Practical Rituals *(Harper & Row, 1985), Teish gathers folk tales in Africa, Australia, the Caribbean, and the southern United States.*

THE BELL OF DOJOJI

Brenda Wong Aoki

This story comes from an ancient Kabuki play with an old theme: unrequited love. I rewrote it from the perspective of women who love too much.

Long ago at the edge of a great forest there was a modest little inn. The innkeeper had a beautiful young daughter named Kiyo, who had been taught ever since she was a tiny little girl to think nothing of herself. Her responsibility was to bring joy to others. So she cooked and scrubbed, working hard every day to bring happiness to those around her. Every night, after serving a visitor his supper, Kiyo would say, "I hope my humble efforts have pleased you." The visitor would invariably respond, "*Hai! Doomo.* Thank you." Kiyo would be pleased, knowing she had done her duty.

Kiyo was at that moment in life when a girl becomes a woman. Her plump ripe body was in the spring of life. Her red lips were soft and full. Sometimes when her work had been particularly tiring, she would fall into the deep slumber of exhaustion and dream a dream of a handsome young man with deep, fathomless eyes, and she would say to him, "I hope my humble efforts have pleased you." He would reply, "*Hai! Doomo.* Thank you."

But before she could say, "Your happiness is my happiness," he would step toward her and encircle her in his arms. His arms were brown and powerful, and they held her tight all night long until she and the young man became one.

So it was that one day Anchin, a monk from Dojoji on a pilgrimage from shrine to shrine, stumbled out of the forest near the inn. The innkeeper, seeing the monk with his begging bowl, invited him to stay and eat.

Now, Anchin happened to be a handsome young man with deep, fathomless eyes. Loving no one, he seldom spoke, and he never listened. Tall and dark, he had learned early on that if he kept silent and left quickly, life was easy. His good looks and inaccessible manner attracted many women. Seeing the reflection of their own desires in his eyes, they followed him. But scorning their praise, sickened by their adulation, Anchin had decided to run away from the world and women and become a monk.

Throwing himself into his studies, he had soon become the most brilliant scholar in the temple. Exhausting himself with physical discipline, his body had become lean and hard. Yet for years the head abbot had watched Anchin and been filled with sadness. One day the head abbot had called Anchin into his chambers.

"Anchin," he said, "you are not a scholar; you are hiding in your books. You are not disciplining your body; you are glorifying it. It is time you left Dojoji and took a lesson in life. Go forth and learn. But never forget to thank those who do you kindness on your journey."

So it was that Anchin found himself at the inn, and kind little Kiyo served him supper. Seeing her own loneliness reflected in his eyes, she thought, *The poor young man! How sad he looks. I will make him happy.* So Kiyo put on a kimono of crimson and silver, unfurled her gilded fan, and danced songs of love. When she was finished, she turned with burning cheeks and sparkling eyes to Anchin. He arose from the table, bowed stiffly, and left without a word.

The next morning Kiyo dressed in her loveliest purple silk kimono, a gift from her father on her 16th birthday. She wrapped a black and silver obi around her slender waist and brought breakfast to Anchin's room. But it was empty—Anchin had gone.

Overcome with sadness, Kiyo crumpled to the floor. But then she remembered the loneliness she had seen reflected in Anchin's eyes and reasoned, "The poor young man! Unable to pay us, he must have left in great embarrassment. I will go and tell him that he is welcome here always." So Kiyo slipped on her scarlet thonged clogs and set out on the path after Anchin. The neighbors smiled as she went her way because Kiyo was such a lovely sight.

Finally catching up with Anchin, she said, "Anchin, don't be ashamed of your begging bowl. Please come back to the inn. Renew your strength. Your happiness is my happiness."

Anchin replied "*Hai! Doomo.* Thank you." And he took a step toward her. Kiyo's heart quickened as she remembered her dream. But just before he seemed about to take her in his arms, he turned abruptly and continued down the path.

Startled and hurt, Kiyo followed him. Mile after mile she followed. Branches tore her silken gown. Her jeweled hair ornaments fell out, but she was so afraid of losing sight of him that she dared not stop to retrieve them.

Faster and faster she went, until her velvet thongs broke, and she tumbled head over heels down a steep ravine. When she regained consciousness, Anchin was standing over her. His eyes reflected worry and concern.

Clutching his leg to her breast, Kiyo looked up into his handsome face and cried, "Anchin, oh, Anchin! Don't worry about me. Now that you're beside me, I feel no pain."

But Anchin shoved her away and said, "I have taken a vow of celibacy. Go back to your father where you belong. You threaten my purity." Again Kiyo reached for him, but he slapped her delicate face and continued on his way.

Alone in the forest, Kiyo stared at her bruised and bleeding hands and thought, *He does love me. He only pretends that he doesn't care because the depth of his passion frightens him.* Strengthened by that thought, Kiyo clawed her way out of the ravine and continued after him. Branches tore her face and grabbed her hair as if the very gods were keeping her from him.

Suddenly the wind rose up, and a strange woman appeared, wearing a torn and soiled chrysanthemum kimono, her face obscured by wild, unbound hair. She glided toward Kiyo and slowly ascended into the air. Like burning coals her eyes glowed in the darkness, and an eerie voice issued from her white lips.

"Kiyo! Kiyo! Kiyo! You are standing at the gateway of Jigoku! She who passes will lose her soul to a lower life form. Anchin is but an illusion. Wake up! Wake up from the dream before you are lost for a hundred existences." The woman faded away like a ghost on the night air.

Kiyo looked around her, and for a moment she could see clearly. The wind sighed through the pines and caressed her brow as if to say, "Kiyo, rest now, and I will soothe your soul." The cicadas sang their brave little song: "Kiyo, we are here only for a moment. Listen to us, and our song will give you strength."

Kiyo saw that her beautiful kimono, the gift of her father, was in tatters. For a moment she realized that she was lost, and she longed for her father. But then she looked up and saw Anchin retreating through the pines.

A fog swirled around her. The cicadas became silent, and Kiyo was blind to everything and everyone but Anchin. Like one possessed, she ran after him.

On and on they ran. At last Anchin reached Dojoji. Standing outside the gate, he cried to his brothers to let him in. The monks looked down from the temple walls and saw that Anchin was pursued by a hideous woman. Her eyes bulged from their sockets. Saliva hung on her lips, and her hair blew about her in tangled clumps.

Quickly the gates were opened, and the head abbot beckoned Anchin to stand beneath the great temple bell. His brother monks, straining and straining, lowered the bell until it fell with a mighty clang, imprisoning Anchin safely within its thick bronze walls.

In rushed Kiyo. Shrieking Anchin's name to the very heavens, she threw herself upon the bell, embracing it with her body. Moaning

Anchin's name and panting, she crawled about it. Her purple robes flowed over it, glittering with a thousand golden scales. Flames burst from her lips. Her tender thighs closed forever and became the long, sinuous tail of a magnificent serpent.

Kiyo wound and coiled herself about the bell of Dojoji and lashed it with her serpent's tail till the bronze was red hot. Still she lashed it, while Anchin cried piteously for mercy. All night long the cicadas sang, and the wind sighed in the pines, but the snake woman on the bell of Dojoji lashed it furiously with her tail until dawn.

In the morning the monks found that the magnificent serpent had disappeared—never to become human again. When the bell was cool enough to touch, they lifted it up. All that remained of Anchin was a little pile of black ash.

Brenda Wong Aoki of San Francisco is the foremost nationally recognized Asian-American storyteller. Her performances blend song, dance, and drama. Aoki recently received funding from the Rockefeller Foundation to develop The Queen's Garden, *a one-woman show based on street stories from her youth in Los Angeles.*

WORK IS WORK

Lynn Rubright

Goodie stirred the porridge pot. Baby patted the pig. The table was set with cream, butter, and cider. Bowls were ready for supper. All was peaceful until Papa came in from working all day in the fields. His hands were blistered, his face was red, his shirt was drenched with sweat.

"Ah, husband, put your scythe in the shed, and wash up for supper. Fresh water's in the bucket by the well."

"Hmph," grumbled Papa. "Look at you, Goodie, with nothing to do but stir porridge for supper. Now, plowing, planting, pulling weeds, and harvesting grain for the miller—that's work, my dear. You wouldn't look so peaceful and rested if you'd been out in the fields like me."

Goodie left the spoon in the stirring pot and stared at her husband. "You think my chores are easier than yours?"

Papa threw back his head and laughed. "You dare compare *my* work with that of a woman at home?"

"Well, then," said Goodie with a smile, "if you work so hard, tomorrow take a rest. I'll tend the fields while you stay at home and play at woman's work for a day."

Papa tickled Baby and smiled. "Switch work?" he said. "We'll do it! Imagine comparing my labors with those of a woman in the home."

Bright and early next day Goodie took the scythe from the shed. She headed down the road, after getting breakfast and tending Baby, of course.

When she was gone, Papa said, "Let's see. Woman's work. I wonder what comes first. I guess I'll churn the butter." He poured sweet cream into the churn and began to beat it. "This butter is slow in coming. Does it always take so long? I'll go down to the cellar for a drink of cider while I rest my arms." But as he opened the tap on the barrel, he heard a terrible crash overhead.

Forgetting the cider flowing from the barrel, he ran up the stairs.

This story, adapted from an old Norwegian folk tale, tells us what happens when a husband stays home to tend the baby and his wife goes out to work in the fields. The tale celebrates the importance of traditional "women's work" and gets across the idea that all work is important, no matter who does it.

49

Baby and pig were slipping and sliding in a puddle of cream on the floor. "Rats! Now that cream will never be butter!" Papa was so mad that he grabbed the pig and threw it out the door.

But poor pig—it hit its head on a rock and fell dead. Baby began to cry. "There now, we'll get another," said Papa. He gave Baby a pat on the head. "Here, chew on this crust. Even without butter, Mama's bread is the best around. Now, be a good girl while I milk the cow in the shed."

Papa brought in fresh milk and put the bucket on the windowsill to cool. "Oh, the cider!" he cried. Papa ran down to the cellar as the last drop of cider dripped onto the floor.

Then he remembered the cow. She needed feeding. Out of breath, he raced upstairs. "It's too late to take her to pasture. I'll just put the cow on the roof. She can graze on the grass growing out of the thatch. Since this house is built next to the hillside, there'll be no trouble getting the cow onto the roof. The only problem will be keeping her there. Imagine a cow grazing on a thatch roof. Your mother never thought of that!"

Papa picked up Baby and hugged her. But the mention of Mama brought new cries from Baby. "Here, drink some fresh milk, and stop fussing while I put the cow on the roof."

With a rope Papa led the cow out of the shed. He coaxed her over the hill and pushed her onto the roof of the house.

"Moo!"

"Stop your mooing!" said Papa. "Munch the sweet grass growing out of the thatch."

When Papa came back inside, Baby whimpered. Papa said, "Here, play with this," and he handed her a doll Mama had made from rags.

"Rats! The sun is almost setting, and I haven't started supper." Papa went out to the well for water. But inside the house Baby started to cry. She was hungry.

"Be patient!" said Papa, running in with the bucket. Baby threw the doll into the water. "Now see what you've done. Never you mind. In no time I'll have supper ready."

Suddenly Papa heard a loud mooing and a strange scuffling sound overhead. He ran outside and saw the cow sliding off the roof.

"Wait!" he shouted as he climbed up to stop her. He pulled the cow back up by the rope. Looking around for a way to secure her, he noticed the chimney. "Of course! I'll drop the rope down the flue and tie it to something inside."

When he got inside, Papa grabbed the rope dangling from the chimney and tied it round his leg. "This should keep the cow on the roof while I make porridge for supper."

Papa poured fresh water into the pot, sprinkled in the oats, and stirred. He put the pot in the fireplace to simmer.

"Wah!" Baby wanted her supper *now*.

Papa handed her the mixing spoon. "Here, chew on this for a while."

But the spoon was hot, and Baby shrieked the louder. The noise scared the cow, which fell off the roof. The rope tied to Papa's leg pulled him—swoosh!—up the chimney.

"Help!" cried Papa from the flue.

"Moo!" boomed the cow, hanging by a rope from the roof.

"Wah!" Baby screamed, even louder this time.

Mistress Goodie, walking home from the fields, started running toward the commotion. "Heavens!" cried Goodie when she saw the cow hanging from the roof. With one swoop of the scythe, she cut the rope in two. The cow fell to the ground with a bump.

Goodie looked through the window in time to see Papa fall headfirst out of the chimney flue and into the porridge. Goodie ran in and with one hand pulled Papa out of the pot.

"It looks like a day of rest at home is more trouble than one spent working in the fields," she said.

But Papa said nothing. He couldn't: his mouth was too full of porridge. With her other hand Goodie grabbed Baby and squeezed her. Baby cooed. She was happy once more.

After supper, when Baby had been tucked into bed, Papa butchered the pig. Mama salted the pork for the barrel. Before going to bed, Papa said, "If you don't mind, Goodie, I'd rather plow the fields. I now know that your chores are no easier than mine."

Goodie said, "Cutting the grain is pleasant enough. But as for me, I prefer to stay at home." She showed him her hands, which were covered with new blisters.

Papa noticed that her nose was burned red from the sun. "I guess work is work," he said.

Goodie smiled and shrugged. "It seems to me that no matter what the work or who does it, a lot of the labor is in getting used to it."

The next day Papa went back to the fields, and Goodie stayed home with Baby. Some say that now and again they switched jobs just for the fun of it. But never again was there talk of whose work was easier.

Lynn Rubright is an assistant professor of education at Webster University in St. Louis and a visiting professor of theater at Northwestern University in Evanston, Illinois. A professional storyteller, writer, composer, and workshop leader, she is the co-founder of the St. Louis Storytelling Festival. With her son, Ted Rubright, she wrote and composed the opera Little Red the Folktale Hen: A Musical Circus.

The Fiddler Of Rattlesnake Ridge

David Holt

About a hundred years ago in the mountains of East Tennessee there lived a fiddler named French Cooper. He came from a long line of fiddlers, but everybody said he was the best of them all. Whenever there was a dance, folks always called French, 'cause when he started to play, you couldn't sit still.

Now, if any of the old people were sick or just didn't feel like getting up, they might call on French, and he'd bring his fiddle over and start playing one of those old-time tunes. Right away they'd start feeling better.

The most amazing thing French could do was fiddle the birds out of the trees—and that's what everybody talked about when they mentioned French Cooper. French would get out in the woods and call to the birds with his fiddle, and the birds would answer him back. He'd call again, and the birds would just hop down on the ground in front of him. It was almost like he and the birds could carry on a conversation.

French had a son named Henry, and Henry used to love to watch his daddy fiddle the birds out of the trees. Henry wanted to be a fiddler just like his daddy, and French tried to teach his son everything he knew. But when Henry was only 15 years old, his father passed away and left Henry his fiddle.

After a while Henry began to play for dances too, and after a dance everybody would come up and say, "Henry, you're making a fine fiddler."

Everybody except for Quinton Edwards, that is. He'd wait until the very end, and then he'd come up and say, "Well, Henry, at least your old man had his fiddlin'. Hmph! Saw him fiddle the birds out of the trees once. That's one thing you'll never do."

Now, Quinton was always saying something bad about somebody, but he had said that too many times, and it was starting to make Henry mad. One day Henry was fiddling up in the woods at a place called

I first heard a version of this story from Kathryn Windham. As I began telling it around the Southern mountains, I heard other accounts of the fiddler whose music could charm snakes out of the ground. After discussing it with Kathryn, my associate, Steve Heller, and I began putting together a version of our own.

Rattlesnake Ridge. He just got lost in his music, swaying back and forth with his eyes closed. When he opened his eyes, he saw a big rattlesnake looking out between the rocks at him. He stopped, and that rattlesnake went back in its hole.

Henry felt like maybe his music had brought the snake out of the ground. He started to play again, and sure enough, that snake came out a second time and stared at him. When Henry stopped fiddling, the snake went back in its hole. Henry was so excited, he just threw his fiddle in the case and started running down the hill toward the house.

Well, Silas, old man Caldwell, and Quinton Edwards were sitting in front of the general store, whittling, when they saw Henry coming by.

Quinton said, "Hey, Henry, what's your hurry?"

Henry stopped long enough to say, "Well, I was up in the woods, and I fiddled a snake out of the ground." Then he rushed straight home and told his mama what had happened. She said, "Why, that's wonderful. You're starting to get some of the magic your daddy had, and I know he'd be proud of you."

The next morning Henry had to go to the store to get some things for his mama. Silas, old man Caldwell, and Quinton were out in front, whittling again.

"Hey, snake charmer, where's your fiddle?" said Quinton.

Henry just ignored him and went into the store. But when he came out, Quinton yelled after him, "Bring us a snake sometime, Henry." Then he laughed.

Henry had heard about all he wanted to from Quinton Edwards, and on his way home he decided he'd surprise that bully. When evening came, he got his fiddle and climbed up to Rattlesnake Ridge again. He found himself a big rock to sit on, took his fiddle out of the case, and tuned it up. Then he started playing an old lonesome tune that he thought might bring the snakes out of the ground.

Henry fiddled for about 15 minutes—just got lost in the music. When he opened his eyes, he saw a great big rattlesnake looking out between the rocks, right at him. Then he saw another and another, until there were seven of the biggest rattlesnakes he had ever seen, just staring at him.

Well, he had done it. He had fiddled the snakes out of the ground. Now he wanted to see if he could make them stretch out in front of him, so he played the tune a little faster. Sure enough, one by one those snakes stretched out of their holes in front of Henry like they were hypnotized. Henry played for them for a long time. Then he thought that maybe if he slowed the music down, they would go back into their holes. So he played a little slower and a little slower and a little slower. One by one they all started to turn around to crawl back to their holes.

When the last snake turned around, Henry jumped up, stepped on its head, pulled out his knife, and cut its head off. Then he picked up the snake's body, threw it in an old tote sack, and climbed down the ridge in darkness.

The next afternoon after Henry had finished his chores, he picked up his fiddle, slung the sack over his shoulder, and walked down to the store. There they were as usual, Quinton, Silas, and old man Caldwell, sitting in front, whittling. Henry walked right up to them, pulled the snake out of his sack, and dropped it in the wood chips at Quinton's feet.

Nobody moved or made a sound.

Finally Quinton said, "Mmm. Suppose you charmed this out of the ground."

"Yes, I did, Quinton Edwards," Henry said. "Up on Rattlesnake Ridge."

"Aw, Henry, you could've gotten this anywhere."

Henry said, "I fiddled it out of the ground, Quinton, up on

Rattlesnake Ridge, and I can do it again."

"Well, do it again, right now, snake charmer," said Quinton. "Bring us a big one."

Old man Caldwell said, "Now, Henry, you don't have to prove nothin' to nobody."

But Henry stood up straight, stared Quinton square in the eye, and said, "Listen out for my fiddle. I won't stop till I bring you that big snake." Then he turned and walked up toward the ridge.

About the time the sun set behind Rattlesnake Ridge, the men heard Henry's fiddling drifting down the wind. Silas, old man Caldwell, and Quinton stopped their whittling for a minute and listened.

Up on the ridge Henry was playing with a vengeance, and there was dark magic in his music. At last he opened his eyes and saw snakes coming out from everywhere—too many to count. The snakes were all around him, but he kept right on playing. Darkness fell, and the men at the store kept on whittling and listening to Henry's fiddle off in the distance.

Finally old man Caldwell said, "You know, young Henry's playing reminds me of ol' French's fiddling." Just about then, the moon came up over Rattlesnake Ridge, and the fiddling stopped.

"Well," Quinton said, "I guess Henry got tired of lookin' for his snake. We'll see him tomorrow if he ain't afraid to show his face." The men said goodnight and went their separate ways in the darkness.

The next morning old man Caldwell sent Silas over to Henry's place to make sure he had come home all right. But his mama told Silas that she hadn't seen her son since the afternoon before, and she was worried. So old man Caldwell, Silas, and Quinton set out for Rattlesnake Ridge to look for Henry.

When they reached the top of the ridge, they came around a big rock—and there was Henry, lying facedown on the ground, his fiddle crushed beneath his chest. He was covered with rattlesnake bites.

Quinton fell to his knees beside Henry's body and whispered, "What have I done?"

Nowadays if you go to that section of woods around Rattlesnake Ridge, folks will say that sometimes at night you can hear something up there. The young people will tell you it's just somebody's radio or TV echoing through the valley. But the old folks, the ones who really know how to listen, will say, "Listen there—that's the ghost of Henry Cooper, fiddlin' for his snakes."

David Holt of Fairview, North Carolina, is an award-winning musician, storyteller, and television personality. He is frequently featured on National Public Radio and the Nashville Network and has appeared on Hee Haw, Nashville Now, *and numerous other programs. His most recent music recording,* Grandfather's Greatest Hits *(High Windy Audio, 1991), features the legendary Chet Atkins, Doc Watson, and Duane Eddy.*

NOT ALONE

Steve Sanfield

My Lithuanian grandfather gave me the gift of stories, but he gave and taught me much, much more. He instilled in me the idea that our ultimate goal is the truth and that in its pursuit we should never let mere facts get in the way. How did he do that? Listen to this tale.

I was 6 years old when I first heard about the imps. Every Tuesday night my grandfather used to come to our house for dinner, and each time he would bring me a bag of fresh mohn cookies from his bakery. I loved those cookies covered with hundreds of tiny poppy seeds, and if I exerted a little self-control, I could sometimes make them last for two or three days.

One Tuesday, however, my grandfather arrived without the cookies. Having come to expect them as part of his visit, I blurted out, "Where are my cookies?" He took a moment to answer and, in a tone much more solemn than usual, he said, "I put aside the best of them for you, but when I went to get them, they were gone. I guess the imps must have taken them." My parents didn't say anything, nor did I. I simply accepted his explanation, just as I accepted everything else he said, and that seemed to be the end of it.

But a few months later, when he came empty-handed again and said it was because of the imps, I said, "What imps?" Not that I was unfamiliar with imps—or even demons, for that matter. After all, my grandfather had been telling me about them for years—with stories about imps all the way from those who were no more than practical jokers to Asmodeus, the King of the Demons himself. But now it was different. They were beginning to affect my own life, for here I was, once again deprived of my precious cookies.

My grandfather took me into the living room, and we sat together on the couch. "I'll tell you about them," he began. "You see, when I was a young man in Vilna, I apprenticed myself to Schlomo the baker. There was no better baker in the entire city. Everything I know I learned from him. After a while he came to trust me completely, so I often found myself alone in the bakery late at night, getting everything ready for the next day.

"Well, one night these two characters appeared as if out of nowhere.

They looked like everybody else except they were smaller, much smaller. Why, they were no bigger than you. Grown men with beards but the size of children. 'Who are you? What are you doing here?' I asked.

"'Who are we?' they said, laughing in squeaky voices. 'We are who we are, and we've come for bread.'

"I told them the bakery wasn't open yet, but if they needed it right then, I could sell them a loaf.

"'A loaf, a loaf,' one of them chanted. 'Did you hear that? The fool says a loaf.'

"The other one joined in, 'A loaf, a loaf—a loaf is for people. We want 20 loaves.'

"I was astonished. 'Twenty loaves! What do you want with 20 loaves?' I asked them. That was all I had baked. Besides, I told them it would cost a lot of money.

"Well, when they heard that, they began to giggle and sing, 'Money, money—money is for fools. We never use money. We just want the bread.'

"I didn't know what to think. I didn't know what to say, so I didn't say anything. I just stood there like a dunce, staring at these two characters. Then they went to the bread rack and started stuffing the loaves under their arms. I tried to stop them. I had to. Schlomo trusted me, and the bakery was my responsibility. I grabbed the loaves from one and put them back on the rack, but as I was doing that, the other one was busy filling his arms. We went on like that for what seemed an eternity: them grabbing, me grabbing back, them grabbing again, until I was so exhausted, I couldn't go on.

"Finally they helped themselves and left with their arms full, singing, 'Money, money—money is for fools.'

"Of course, when Schlomo came in just before dawn, I immediately told him what had happened. He slapped his forehead and groaned, '*Oy gevalt!* I should have told you about them. They come to the bakery every now and then, and I always let them have whatever they want. Sometimes I don't see them for years. Sometimes they're back in a week. It was that way in my father's time, and it's been that way ever since I've been here. My father told me they were imps and should never be questioned. Giving them what they want is much easier than not. I just hope you haven't done something terrible. Who knows what will happen now?'

"That's what Schlomo told me," my grandfather continued, "but the fact is, nothing happened, at least not while I was there, and that was more than two years. Then I came here to America. I worked in other bakeries and saved my money until I had enough to open my own. That's when I began to see them again.

"Actually, I didn't really see them at first, but I knew they had followed me all the way across the ocean. All kinds of crazy things would happen. I'd be out front with a customer, and suddenly there'd be a big crash from the back. A rack would be on the floor, rolls scattered everywhere. Sometimes when I was in the middle of boiling bagels, the fire under the big copper kettle would just go out. And many times when I'd bake a special order, say, a cake for a bar mitzvah or a wedding, it would simply vanish. Poof! Just like that. I didn't have to see them to know they were there.

"After a while they began to show their faces. It was them, all right, the same two. I'd see them going out the back door, loaded down with all kinds of stuff, or I'd hear them singing that same song they sang that night back in Vilna: 'Money, money—money is for fools.' But they've never let me get close, and they've never spoken to me. I guess that's what happened to your mohn cookies," my grandfather concluded.

Of course, I took this to be the absolute truth. I never questioned any of my grandfather's other stories. Why should I question this one? The presence of imps in his bakery seemed perfectly natural to me.

Much to my relief, they never came up again, because from that night on, whenever my grandfather came to visit, he always brought me a bag of mohn cookies. Even when he retired from baking and took to selling those little white labels that used to appear on loaves of rye and pumpernickel and challah, proclaiming that not only was this bread kosher but union-made as well, he never forgot the cookies.

Years later I was home from college and went to visit him. On the way to my uncle's house, where he was living, I passed a Jewish bakery, and something made me stop. Inside all was familiar. There were the breads and rolls and pastries of my childhood, and there in one of the cases was a tray of mohn cookies. I bought a dozen and took them as a gift to my grandfather. As we were eating them along with our tea (mine in a cup, his in a glass), I asked him what had happened to the imps.

"Ah," he said, with a twinkle in his eye, "you remember them. Well, they kept up their tricks for years. I finally accepted what they did. It seemed to be my fate, and who am I to question mysteries I don't understand? But one time—it happened when my helper was in the hospital for an operation of some kind or another, and I had to do everything alone—they began to come every night. They'd open the ovens, spoil batches of dough, turn over this and that, and of course, take whatever they pleased. I thought I'd go crazy.

"Enough is enough, and so one night I screamed at them, 'Why do you torment me so? What I did in Vilna, I did. I was a young man. I didn't know any better. I'm sorry. I'm sorry.'

"'Sorry, sorry. The fool says he's sorry,' one of them sang. With that they dropped the rolls they were carrying and walked right up to me. Then they spoke to me for the first time in 35 years. They told me I'd made an awful mistake back there in Vilna. They said that imps don't ask for very much, and it's important that they be given what they do ask for. We humans must understand that we are not alone in this world. There are all kinds of creatures, and each has its own place and purpose. It's not always given to us to understand what that might be, and for us to think we can have control over everything is pure foolishness. 'The silly pride of people,' the imps called it.

"They talked, and I listened, and when they finished, I promised to give them whatever they wanted, whenever they wanted it. I even told them I'd bake special treats for them. And you know something?" my grandfather said with a laugh. "I never saw them again."

Steve Sanfield is a prize-winning author, a poet, and one of America's most respected tellers of Jewish tales. His books include The Adventures of High John the Conqueror *(Orchard Books, 1989) and* The Feather Merchants and Other Tales of the Fools of Chelm *(Orchard Books, 1991). The founder and artistic director of the Sierra Storytelling Festival, Sanfield lives outside Nevada City, California.*

Uncle Bouqui
and Godfather Malice

Augusta Baker

One time Bouqui and Malice were farming together in the Red Mountains. Every day they went out to their fields with their hoes and machetes, and they worked until the middle of the afternoon, when the sun was broiling hot.

Uncle Guinéda, who lived in the village, had chopped down a tree full of honey, and he gave Bouqui a big gourd full of it because Bouqui was godfather to Guinéda's youngest child. Bouqui was very proud and jealous of that gourd of honey, and he hung it up in the rafters of his house, intending to save it for a big holiday, such as Christmas or Dessaline's Day.

Now, Ti Malice liked honey just about better than anything. His mouth watered at the sight of that gourd hanging there in the rafters. Four or five times he politely suggested that they sit down and have a glass of honey, but Bouqui shook his head and made an ugly face.

"I'm saving that honey for an occasion," Bouqui said.

"When two good friends get together, that *is* an occasion," Malice said.

"Do you think I'm a rich man?" Bouqui said. "I can't eat honey every day."

One hot morning they were out in the field, cultivating corn. The earth was dry, and the sun was hot, and Malice became thirstier and thirstier. He began to think of that cool gourd of honey hanging in the rafters of Bouqui's house. Two or three times he stood very still and closed his eyes just so he could imagine the honey.

Finally he dropped his hoe on the ground.

"Wah!" he said. "Someone is calling me."

"I didn't hear anything but a lamb *baaing*," Bouqui said, "and it didn't sound like *Malice*."

"Wah! There it is again," Malice said. "I'll have to go see who it is."

He picked up his hat and marched over the hill, and when he was

*Fifty years ago
I was introduced to
Harold Courlander's
collection of Haitian
tales,* Uncle Bouqui
of Haiti *(Morrow,
1942). They were
lively, humorous, full
of action and colorful
language. The two
main characters are
Uncle Bouqui—large,
kindly, slow-thinking,
always in trouble—
and Ti Malice, a little
troublemaker who
never stops thinking
and scheming.
These are still my
favorite stories.*

out of Bouqui's sight, he turned and headed for Bouqui's house. He went inside and climbed up into the rafters and took down the honey gourd. He poured some honey into a glass, mixed it with water, and drank it. Then he mixed some more and drank it. He kept mixing and drinking until he was so full that he couldn't swallow another drop. Then he hung the gourd back in the rafters and returned to the field.

Bouqui was working away with his hoe, and he was mighty hot. He pushed out his lips and made an ugly face.

"You certainly were gone long enough. What happened to you?"

"Wah, Bouqui! Everyone wants me to be godfather to his children. Nobody leaves me alone. I had to go to a baptism."

"Woy, that's different!" Bouqui said, breaking into a smile. "Is it a boy or girl?"

"A girl, and a very nice one indeed," Malice said, licking the honey off his chin.

"Wonderful!" Bouqui said, beaming and resting his arms on the hoe handle. "I like babies. What's her name?"

"Her name?" Malice said. "Oh yes. Well, I named her Début." (*Début* means "beginning" in Creole.)

"Début!" Bouqui gasped. "Woy, what an elegant name. How did you ever think of it?"

"It just came to me," Ti Malice said modestly. And he picked up his hoe and went back to work.

The next day they were weeding the garden with their machetes, and the sun got hotter and hotter, and Malice got thirstier and thirstier. He tried to keep his mind on his work, but all he could think of was that honey gourd hanging in Uncle Bouqui's rafters. Suddenly he stood up straight and cocked his ear and said, "Wah, Bouqui, did someone call me?"

"I don't think so," Bouqui answered. "I heard a calf bawling on the next hill, but I don't think he mentioned your name."

"There!" Malice said. "There it is again! I'll have to go see who wants me." He stuck his machete into his belt and marched over the hill.

Bouqui shook his head and mumbled to himself. He rapped his right ear with his knuckles, and then he took hold of his left ear and tweaked it.

"My ears are asleep," he said. "I didn't hear a thing."

As soon as he was out of sight, Malice turned and ran for Bouqui's house. He climbed up into the rafters and brought down the honey gourd and fixed himself a big drink. He fixed another and another. He drank and drank and drank until he felt ready to burst. Then he hung the gourd in the rafters again and went down to the field where Bouqui was chopping away in the hot sun.

"Well, what happened?" Bouqui asked impatiently. "You were gone a tremendously long time."

"Uncle Bouqui, my friends just won't leave me alone. They're always bothering me. It's always Malice this and Malice that. They needed me to come and baptize another baby."

"That's a different matter," Bouqui said with a grin. "Boy or girl?"

"A boy this time," Malice said, licking honey off his fingers.

"What's his name?" Bouqui said. "I certainly like babies."

"His name. Oh, well, I called this one Dèmi," Malice said. (*Dèmi* means halfway in Creole.)

"Dèmi! What a fine name! You certainly have a wonderful imagination. Dèmi! It's mighty sweet."

"It certainly is," Malice answered. "There's probably just one more as sweet as that one." And they picked up their machetes and went back to work.

The next day they were out cultivating again. The sun got hotter and hotter. Malice started to sing to keep his mind off the honey, but it was no use. He threw his hoe down on the ground.

"Wah!" he said. "What an imposition!"

"What's the matter?"

"Didn't you hear?" Malice said.

"No, only some dogs barking."

"Someone's calling me again. What do you think he wants?"

"People certainly are having babies!" Bouqui said. "Don't be gone long!" He twisted and jerked his ears. "They're half dead," he muttered. "I didn't hear anything but the dogs."

Malice headed over the hill, and then he scrambled for Uncle Bouqui's house. He took down the honey gourd and drank and drank. He drank until the gourd was empty. He stuck his tongue inside and licked it clean as far as he could reach. When he was through, the gourd was dry as an old cornstalk. He hung it up in the rafters and went back to where Uncle Bouqui was sweating and making dark faces in the hot sun.

"Well," Bouqui said, "what was it?"

"Another baby," Ti Malice said. "A girl. I think it's the last one."

"Wonderful!" Bouqui said. "What did you name it?"

"Name it? Oh. Well, I named this one Sêche," Malice said. (*Sêche* means "dry" in Creole.)

"Sêche! What an unusual name," Bouqui said. "Woy, you are just about the best baby-namer in Haiti."

When they went home after work that night, Bouqui said, "You know, I think we should celebrate all those babies tonight. Why should I save the honey until Christmas? If we don't drink it, the flies will."

He reached up in the rafters and took down the gourd. He stood there a long time looking into it. Then he carried it outside and looked again. He closed his eyes for a minute, then opened them. He turned the gourd upside-down, but nothing happened. He licked the edges, but they didn't even taste like honey. He smelled the gourd, but there wasn't even an odor left.

"Oh-oh!" he said at last. "It's gone."

He turned around, but somehow Malice seemed to have disappeared too. Uncle Bouqui sat down to think. He thought, thought, thought. He mumbled and argued with himself. He scratched his head first, and then he scratched his chin. He just couldn't make any sense out of it. Suddenly he began to tingle. For a moment he sat very still, tingling from head to toe. Then he leaped into the air and howled.

"Wah! The first one was named Début! And the second was named Dèmi! And the third was named Sêche! Beginning, halfway, and dry! Wah!" he wailed. "And all the time I was out there working! Beginning, halfway, and dry—of my honey!"

That night Uncle Bouqui waited until Ti Malice was asleep on his mat, and then he crawled into his house quietly on his hands and knees. "Beginning, halfway, dry," he kept saying over and over to himself. When he got to Malice's mat, Bouqui opened his mouth wide and—*pimme!* He clamped his teeth down hard on Malice's big toe. Malice let out a wild yowl and sprang into the air, but Bouqui hung on.

"Ouch!" Malice yelled. "Stop it; you're killing me!"

Bouqui let go with his teeth, and Malice's yelling died down to a moan.

"Uncle Bouqui!" he whimpered. "Uncle Bouqui! What do you call that, anyway?"

"I call that one Début!" Bouqui shouted. And he lunged forward— *pamme!* He caught Malice's other big toe right between his teeth.

Malice leaped and jerked and howled, but Bouqui held on. Malice hopped and crawled and jumped, but Uncle Bouqui wouldn't let go.

"Wah!" Malice screamed. "I'm hurt for life!"

Bouqui opened his mouth and made a ferocious face at Malice.

"Uncle Bouqui, Uncle Bouqui!" Malice groaned. "What do you call this business, anyway?"

"I call this one Dèmi!" Bouqui shouted. And he lunged forward to get another one of Malice's toes with his teeth.

But Ti Malice came to life. He sprang across the room as though he were running on hot coals. In no time at all he was outside, racing off into the hills.

"Wah!" he howled as he went through the gate. "Wah! There's one thing you'll never do, Bouqui! You'll never be godfather to Sêche! Not unless you catch me first!" And he disappeared into the darkness without another word.

Bouqui stood listening until the sound of Malice's feet slapping against the trail had died away. He got to thinking.

"Sêche," he said. "It's a mighty unusual name, at that."

Augusta Baker is the storyteller-in-residence at the University of South Carolina at Columbia's College of Library and Information Science. Considered America's first lady of traditional storytelling, she is a former coordinator of children's services for the New York Public Library. Baker is the co-author of Storytelling: Art and Technique *(R.R. Bowker, 1977).*

GOODBYE TO EDEN

Gwenda LedBetter

I grew up in sound and sight of the sea. The Atlantic Ocean and the Chesapeake Bay converged and met at the end of the peninsula where I lived, in a small town called Cape Charles, Virginia. The ferry from Norfolk spilled cars and people onto a dock that smelled of creosote. I still love that nose-stretching smell. At the wharf was a roundhouse, where the Pennsylvania Railroad ended its run. The air was filled with train whistles and the screeching of wheels on the rails. Seagulls squawked overhead, and at the end of a rock jetty, a bell buoy sang its lonesome *dong, dong* all through the Cape Charles day.

Cape Charles was a small railroad town, laid out in a grid, and all the streets coming into town from the highway ended up at the beach. We lived in an upstairs apartment on Tazewell Avenue, about 90 steps from the water. I'd stand at the porch railing, just barely able to peer over and look at the bay as it stretched and stretched until it met the sky.

I thought the presence of water was an always kind of thing, like the ground under your feet. It stayed where it was. Then we had a storm: the hurricane of 1933. And when I went out on the porch, I saw the bay pouring over the boardwalk in a great waterfall and someone's rowboat floating in our yard. I felt betrayed when I realized that things change. They don't stay the same.

But oh, how I loved that town. Those were the Depression years, and pleasures were simple. We could go to the movies for a nickel, if we had a nickel. We'd have picnics on the beach. We'd swim until we were slick as fish, then someone would call, "Come on out! Time to eat."

I'd put on my father's shirt, which dragged the ground, and head for the food: Chicken fried golden brown. Deviled eggs, wrapped in wax paper, twisted at the ends. And brownies. They made the word *chocolate* what it is for me today. The food would disappear, and our neighbor Annie Jarvis would say, "I'll never fit into my girdle again." (We all agreed.)

Once someone asked me if I had a "goodbye story." I said no, but later I remembered my first-grade teacher, Miss Becky Scott, and having to leave the town I'd loved like none other. What Miss Scott did for me was probably not unusual, but I was mighty lucky to have her in my life.

69

The sun would slide down into that blue silk water, striping it with rose and gold, and someone would build a fire. We'd roast marshmallows as the sky turned royal blue and the stars came out. The sand felt cold on my hot skin, and people would tell stories and sing, harmonizing whether they could or not. People's faces seemed to float there among the sparks, and when I looked up, I couldn't tell the sparks from the stars. Underneath the voices was the constant wash of the waves on sand. I never lasted past the second marshmallow and would go home with my head on my father's shoulder.

I had three special girlfriends: Millie, Joanne, and Peggy. Then there was Tommy Kellam, who lived next door. He and I were always together. The Jarvises lived across the street. Annie laughed as much as she ate. It made me feel good just to be near their house. I'd sit on the back steps underneath the grape arbor and listen to Annie and the canary in the kitchen. She'd look out the window and ask, "What you doing out there, honey?"

"Just sittin', Annie."

"Well, you just sit all you want to." Then I'd hear the wonderful sound of her laughter. It was like bubbles and getting tickled in all the right places. It made everything even better than it already was.

Life was good. Then came the first day of school.

I'd been going to my mother's Wee Wisdom kindergarten for three years, but now I'd be attending a big school. Tommy and I got new book bags. Mother pulled my Shirley Temple curls into pigtails. Tommy's hair was water-slick smooth. We were both so clean we looked peeled.

The school was only two blocks away, and we walked down the sidewalk, which was broken in places, with the grass showing through. We passed a boxwood hedge, turned the corner, and walked up the steps into Miss Becky Scott's first grade.

When I saw Miss Scott, it was love at first sight. She was a tall woman. I kept looking up and up and still up into her kind face. She wore her hair in a single braid, wrapped around her head in what was called a coronet. To me it *was* a crown, for she became my queen, my goddess of learning.

Miss Scott taught us that life can be summed up in words, and words can turn into life. We sat in a half-circle in our little blue chairs and practiced that magic chant:

See Dick run.
See Jane run.
See Spot run, and
See Puff run.

And they ran and jumped all over the page, as if our saying the words had made them do it.

One day I came home from school to find things all gone wrong. My father was home at the wrong time of day, and my mother's nose and eyes were red from crying. They said to me, "We have to move."

Move? I couldn't understand it. Why would you want to leave a place you loved? Why would you want to leave Eden? If there ever was one, that town was Eden to me.

Dad was to go on to a new town, 50 miles up the road, and Mother and I would follow on the bus when school let out for the year. Soon it was time to say goodbye—to Millie, Joanne, and Peggy; to Tommy, who seemed like a part of me; to the Jarvises (Annie didn't laugh at all); and to Miss Becky Scott.

I wanted to give Miss Scott a present. It was traditional in the first grade. Besides, she was my queen, and I might not ever see her again. Mother helped me pick out a vase. It was green pottery and the right size and shape to hold daisies or daffodils. Mother said she'd get plenty of both. I was to carry it to her. I remember how the clay felt in my hands as I carried the vase straight out in front of me, the way one carries gifts to royalty.

I had just passed the boxwood hedge when my toe caught in one of the cracks in the sidewalk. I tripped and watched the vase do an endless loop in the air, winding up on the sidewalk as a picture puzzle of a green vase. I must have been in shock. Instead of crying and running back home, I picked up two or three of the pieces and kept on walking to the school.

When I got to Miss Scott's room, she was sitting behind her desk. The room smelled of chalk, that oiled dust the janitor used to sweep the floors with, and the essence of 7-year-old bodies. Miss Scott looked up.

"Why, Gwenda—I thought you had already left town."

Then the tears came, pouring out like the bay over the boardwalk, accompanied by sobs that made me feel as though I was going to split wide open. Miss Scott came running over, stooped down to put her arm around me, and found the pieces of the vase.

"Was this for me?"

I nodded my head, splashing us both with tears. I sniveled and hiccuped out the story, and Miss Scott said, "Well, it's a strange thing, but I've been needing something like this to put in the bottoms of my flowerpots."

She walked me over to her desk, where she put down the pieces of broken vase with infinite care, as if they were shards from some ancient civilization. Then her face brightened.

"Gwenda, I have something to show you," she said. "Let's go to the science corner."

When we got there, she told me to cup my hands together and close my eyes. I did, and then I felt something small and soft and incredibly alive. I opened my eyes to find that I was holding a tiny chick. Miss Scott stooped down, put her arm around me, and stroked the chick's head.

"I know you don't want to leave Cape Charles, Gwenda. You love it here. And you probably will be lonely at first. But I think it will be like this little fellow: it'll be a new life, filled with all kinds of things. It will be a new life indeed."

We put the chick down, and she walked me back to the desk. Miss Scott gave me a book with words I could read and waved me down the steps and into the street.

Two days after that Mother and I got on the bus to leave town. As it went down Tazewell Avenue, all the neighbors came out to say goodbye. I knelt at the window in the back of the bus to look at what I loved for as long as I could. When I could no longer see the water or the waving hands for the chinaberry trees, I turned around to sink down into that end-of-the-world feeling. My hands were lying loose in my lap. Then I remembered how that chick had felt—so small and soft but so full of life. And I thought about Miss Scott's words: "It will be a new life . . . a new life indeed."

I reached for the book full of magic words that she had given me, and I read all the way down the road and into the rest of my life.

Gwenda LedBetter of Asheville, North Carolina, has shared her folk and spiritual narratives with audiences for more than 25 years. She began her storytelling career at Asheville's Pack Library and on WLOS-TV as the Storylady. She has taught at the National Storytelling Institute.

DAUGHTER OF THE SUN

Gayle Ross

I first found this story among the tales collected by ethnologist James Mooney in the late 1800s. It teaches an important lesson about humans' attempting to control natural forces and thus throwing life out of balance. It also speaks to the importance of reconciliation.

The sun is a woman, and she lives in the sky vault in the east. Her brother, the moon, lives in the west. Long ago her daughter lived directly above the earth, and every day as the sun made that long journey across the sky to the west, she would stop at her daughter's house to linger awhile and maybe share dinner.

In those days the sun had no love for the people on Earth because they could never look at her without wrinkling up their faces or squinting their eyes. She said to her brother, the moon, "My grandchildren are so ugly. They frown all over their faces when they look at me." Her light was hot and bright.

But the moon thought the people on Earth were very handsome because they always smiled when they saw the moon in the sky at night. His light was soft and gentle. So the sun grew jealous of the moon.

As the sun's anger and hatred grew, she decided to kill all the people on Earth. Every day when she came near her daughter's house, she let her anger burn fierce and bright, until a great fever spread across the land, and the people began to die.

Soon everyone had lost a loved one, and the people were afraid that before long no one would be left. So they sought the help of two little men, the twin sons of the thunder beings, who lived in the darkening land.

The little men told the people of Earth that the only way to save themselves was to kill the sun. So the little men used their power and changed two people into snakes—one into a spreading adder and the other into a copperhead. Then they sent the two snakes into the sky to hide at the door of the sun's daughter so they might bite the sun when she came to dinner.

When the sun approached her daughter's house, the spreading adder drew up as though to strike, but the bright hot light of the sun blinded him, and he could only spit a yellow slime, as he does to this day when he tries to bite. The sun called him a nasty being and walked by him into her daughter's house, and the adder was ashamed and returned to Earth. After seeing what had happened to the adder, the copperhead crawled away and returned to Earth as well.

The people continued to die, so they went to the little men a second time. Again the little men made their medicine, this time changing one man into a rattlesnake and another into the great Uktena, the spirit serpent of the Cherokees. The Uktena is large and ferocious, with horns on his head, and he was so fierce that everyone thought he would be the one to kill the sun. But the rattlesnake loved the people, and he was eager to be the one to save them.

So he raced ahead and coiled up outside the door of the house of the sun's daughter. When the sun's daughter opened the door to watch for her mother, the rattlesnake struck and bit her, and she fell dead in the doorway. Seeing what he had done, the rattlesnake was ashamed and afraid. He did not wait for the sun but returned to the land of the people. When the Uktena saw what the rattlesnake had done, he too was angry, and he returned to Earth as well.

Today we Cherokees honor the rattlesnake and pray to him and do not kill him, because he is kind and will never bite unless he is disturbed. But the Uktena's anger grew until he became so fierce and dangerous that no man could so much as look him in the face without members of his family dying. Finally the people held a great council, and they decided that the Uktena was too dangerous to live on the land. So they sent him to the sky vault to live, and he is there to this very day.

Now, when the sun found the body of her daughter, her heart broke, and she went into her daughter's house and grieved. And there she stayed. The people weren't dying anymore; instead the world was cold and dark. When the sun refused to come out, the people went again to the little men. They told the people that if they were to see the sun again, they must bring back her daughter from the spirit world—the ghost country—in the darkening land.

The little men chose seven people to go to the darkening land, and to each one they gave a staff of sourwood, carved and polished. The little men told them that when they came to the darkening land, they would find all the spirits of the dead dancing. "When a young woman dances by each of you," they said, "one by one, touch her with your staffs, and she will fall to the ground in a deep sleep. Then you must put her in this box and, as quickly as you can, return to your own country. But you must be very sure not to open the box until you are safely home again.

"Remember," said the little men, "no matter what you hear, no matter what you think, do not open the box until you are home again."

The seven men took their staffs and the box and traveled seven days and seven nights until they came to the spirit world. There they found all the spirits dancing.

As a young woman danced past the seven men, one reached out and touched her with his staff, and she turned her head to look at him. As she continued to dance on by, each of the other men touched her with his staff, and she fell to the ground in a deep sleep. The men quickly put her in the box, closed the lid, and started home.

But after a while the girl woke and began to plead with them to let her out: "Please, please, open the box." The men made no answer and hurried on. Soon she was calling again: "I'm hungry. Please, open the box." They did not pause but instead hastened their steps. After a while she spoke again, calling for a drink. Still they went on.

But at last, when they were very near their own country, the girl called again and begged them to raise the lid just a little. "I'm smothering," she said. "I'm afraid I'll die." The men were also afraid of this, so they lifted the lid just a little to give her some air. As they did, they heard a faint fluttering sound and felt something fly by them into the thicket. Then they heard the sweet, piercing call of a bird's song, and looking into the bushes, they saw a bird unlike any they had ever seen.

The bird's feathers were a deep, rich red—as red as the sun herself when she leaves her home in the east in the early moments of dawn. And when the bird turned in the bushes, they saw that it looked at them with the young woman's eyes. The men hurried home, but when they got there and opened the box, it was empty.

If the men had kept the box closed as they had been told, they could have brought the young woman home safely. And then, perhaps, we could bring back our loved ones from the spirit world. Maybe, maybe not—but to this day we honor the redbird as the daughter of the sun.

The sun had been overjoyed when the men began their journey to the spirit world. But when they came back without her daughter, she grieved anew. She wept until her tears made a flood upon the earth, and the people were afraid that the world would be drowned. So the people held another council, and they sent their most handsome young men and women to sing and dance for the sun so she would stop crying.

The people danced before her and sang their best songs, but for a long time she kept her face covered and would not look at them. Finally the drummer quickened his beat, and a singer began a song with the melody of the redbird's call. When the sun heard the people singing of their love for her daughter, she lifted her face from her hands and saw the people singing and dancing for her. She forgot her grief, and she forgave the people.

The sun returned to her home in the east and resumed her daily journey across the sky vault to the west. To this day the sun and the people love and honor one another. And now at noon, when the sun reaches the highest part of the heavens, she seems to stand very still for just a moment—and the people know she is remembering the days when she could linger at the house of her daughter.

Gayle Ross of Fredericksburg, Texas, is best known for recounting the history and legends of the Cherokee Indians. A direct descendant of John Ross, a principal chief of the Cherokee Nation, she grew up hearing stories from her grandmother. In 1991 Ross's audiotape How Rabbit Tricked Otter *(Parabola, 1991) won the Publishers Marketing Association's Benjamin Franklin Award for best cassette.*

GRANNY GIFTS

Anndrena Belcher

When I was a little girl, I used to like to visit Mamaw Mollie and Granddaddy Glenn. They lived up in a holler called Laurel Branch over on Marrowbone Creek in Pike County, Kentucky. Their house had a big front porch, and it was filled with rocking chairs and one great long swing. After we'd finish our chores during the day, we'd sit on the porch and look out on the beautiful mountains all around us.

Mamaw had a favorite rocking chair, and one day she was sitting in it, rocking real slow back and forth. She had one hand cupped real gentle-like over the other. Well, I got in the swing and started in a-swingin'—wham-bangedy-bang, wham-bangedy-bang, wham-bangedy-bang. Every time I would swing back, I'd hit the wall of the house and make the windows rattle. I guess Mamaw stood that racket as long as she could, and then she looked over at me and said, "Annie, for heaven's sake, do you have to make such a clatter all the time? Can't you swing a little more quiet-like?"

I stopped my swinging right then and there, and I looked at her sitting so peacefully in that chair with her hands folded. I said, "Mamaw, I'm restless inside. I don't know how you can sit there and be so peaceful."

My mamaw had long white hair that reached way down past her bottom, and when we were good little girls, she would let us brush it. Right then she got up from her chair and went into the house, and when she came back out, she had her hairbrush. She handed it to me and said, "Brush my hair, child, and I'll tell you a story about how I come to be so peaceful."

She took the pins out of the bun on top of her head and let that long white hair ripple all down around her shoulders. I started to brush, and she commenced to telling me the story.

"You see, Annie, when I was your age, growing up around here, all the younguns got to go visit this little granny-woman. When you went to

My family moved from the coal fields of Eastern Kentucky to inner-city Chicago when I was in the second grade. Stories and images of home helped me survive, taught me who I am. I've learned to live in my imagination and to take home with me wherever I travel. Step on the yarn-ball string, and you'll see what I mean.

see the granny-woman, she would give you a gift to carry on life's journey. Well, it come my time to go see her, and I didn't know what gift I wanted to ask her for. When I got to her house, she knowed me before I even told her my name, and she asked me, 'Mollie, do you know which gift you want to ask me for?'

"I told her, 'No, ma'am, I don't know what I want to ask you for. I was wondering if you could tell me what you've got.' That old woman went into her house, and she come back out carrying an armful of a ball of green yarn. She threwed it out in front of her and let it unravel through the gap in the mountains, and she said, 'Since you don't know which gift you want, I'm going to send you to the homes of some of your cousins. I have give them gifts the last two or three years, so you go see how they're doing with their gifts, and then come back and tell me what you want for yourself. You just step on this little string—that's how you'll travel. When you've seen what you want to see, pull on the string, and I'll bring you back.'"

My mamaw wasn't used to traveling that way, but she wasn't going to sass that old woman. So she stepped on the string, and the granny-woman told her, "First I am going to send you to see your cousin Vanessa. Vanessa asked me for the gift of beauty."

My mamaw said she stepped on the string and—whoosh—before she could snap her fingers, she stood in front of a house. When she knocked on the door, sure enough, it was her cousin Vanessa who answered. But she looked real different. She knew my mamaw and invited her in. My mamaw said she was speechless. She told me, "Annie, I couldn't say a word. That woman was so beautiful I couldn't talk. There was all kinds of menfolks courting her. There was all kinds of people painting her picture because she was so pretty to look at."

She said, "I stayed there for three days, and I pulled on that little string, and—whoosh—the old woman brung me back to her house just like she said she would. She asked me, 'Well, Mollie, what do you think of the gift of beauty? Is that what you want for yourself, honey?'"

My mamaw told her, "At first I surely did want to look like Vanessa. She was the prettiest woman I'd ever seen, and she had all those menfolks a-courting her and people coming just to admire the way she looked. But while I was there, something awful happened. Vanessa got sick, and when she got sick, all her beauty faded away. All the menfolks who was courting, they've done left, and all the other friends too. And Vanessa, she's done fell out of the use of her imagination, and she don't know what to do to make a living. She wanted me to ask you, could you please give her back the gift of beauty?

"'Oh my. It's a pity, for I can give the gift but once. Vanessa is going to have to figure out another way to get along in life without that gift of beauty.'

"No, I don't think the gift of beauty is what I want. Have you got something else?" This time the old woman went into the house and came out with a red ball of yarn just as big as the first one, and she unraveled it in front of my mamaw. It went through the gap in the mountains. She told Mamaw, "This time, child, I am sending you to see your cousin Cassandra. Cassandra asked me for the gift of eloquence. She said she wanted power through the use of words. Fancy that."

My mamaw said she hadn't ever heard of anything called eloquence, and she didn't know that she would think much of it, but she figured she would go and see. So she stepped on that string, and once again she flew right through the gap in the mountains and landed at a house. When her cousin Cassandra answered the door, Mamaw knew it was her.

Cassandra invited my mamaw in, and then she began to talk so fast that nobody could get a word in edgewise. She talked about dog ticks, lunatics, and politics. My mamaw said she stayed there for three hours, and then she couldn't stand any more. So she pulled on the string, and—whoosh—she was back at the old woman's house. Mamaw's eyes were all puffed out, and she was worn to a frazzle.

The old granny-woman asked her, "Well, child, what did you think of the gift of eloquence? You're not sick, are you? I see them big bags under your eyes."

My mamaw told her, "At first I liked the gift of eloquence, and Cassandra's words were real interesting, and all kinds of people came to listen to her talk. But she never let anybody else talk. She's forgotten how to listen. No, I don't think I want the gift of eloquence. Have you got anything else?"

The old woman went into her house a third time. When she came out, she had a ball of yarn that fit into her little hand. It was golden, and it sparkled all over with emeralds and rubies and diamonds. My mamaw said it was real pretty, and she held out her hand because she thought the old woman was going to give her that ball of yarn as a present. But no, she went ahead and throwed it out in front of her, and it unraveled through the gap in the mountains just like the other two had.

She told Mamaw, "Now I'm going to send you to see your cousin Wealthea."

You can guess what gift Wealthea had asked for. My mamaw said she stepped on that sparkly little string, and she went flying through that gap in the mountains again. She landed in front of a mansion on a hill: a big white house with columns up and down in front of it, a great big circular driveway, a huge swimming pool—even a Ferris wheel. All kinds of long black cars were driving up into the driveway. When their doors opened, out stepped beautiful women in swishy dresses and men wearing funny-looking black-and-white outfits.

Mamaw was excited, and she walked up and knocked on the door. When her cousin Wealthea came to the door, oh, she looked the same as always, but she sounded different. She said to Mamaw, "Oh, Mollie, do come in."

My mamaw went inside that big old house, and Wealthea took her upstairs to a chifforobe that reached up to the ceiling and opened with a pretty little golden key. When Wealthea opened it, there was a whole pile of beautiful, fancy dresses. Wealthea let my mamaw pick out one—a silvery dress that shone just like the moon—and gave her a little crown and some ear-bobs to wear. My mamaw said she went dancing all over that house, and that evening, just like every evening, there was a party. There was a long table filled with all kinds of food—everything you can imagine.

My mamaw stayed there for seven days, and then she pulled on the little string, and—whoosh—she went flying back to the old woman's house, still wearing her silvery dress and her little crown. The granny-woman asked her, "Mollie, have you decided that the gift of wealth is what you want after all? You've been gone a long time."

My mamaw told the old woman, "Well, I certainly had an awful nice time—dancing, swimming in the pool, riding the Ferris wheel, listening to music, eating all that wonderful food, and wearing my beautiful clothes. I thought I was going to ask you for the gift of wealth, but while I was there, something happened. One night while we was getting ready to have one of them dancing parties, there was a knock at the door. The doorman opened the door, and there in the doorway stood a little hunkered-over old woman. She looked like she was a hundred years old. She had a raggedy scarf tied about her head, and her gray hair stuck out from under it kind of wild-like. Well, the doorman asked her, 'May I help you?' She said to him, 'Do you have a job of work for me? I need a job awful bad.'

"'No, we haven't a job of work for you.'

"Then she held out her hand, said, 'Could you spare a piece of bread for my journey?'

"That man swelled up his chest and looked down his nose and said, 'We've hardly enough for ourselves.' And he closed the door on that old woman. Why, there was that table laid with all kinds of food, enough to feed a hundred people.

"No, if getting wealth and keeping it causes you to be that greedy, it's not what I want. I don't even know if you can give me the gift I'm about to ask for. But what I want is the knowledge to understand these things I've seen and experienced. Maybe that understanding will help me to have a peaceful spirit inside. Maybe it'll lead me to work toward bringing peace in my own little corner of the world however I can.

"'Well, Mollie, 'tis a wise child you are to ask for such a gift—and you're so young. Indeed, you possess much of it already.'"

That granny-woman gave my mamaw a special gift, and she sent her to live with a storytelling woman. For storytellers, I understand, tell the kind of tales that try to uncover the truth and hold it out for everybody to learn from. Once you know the truth, you can work toward bringing peace to your little corner of the world, and that's what gives you peace inside.

My mamaw said that's what brought her to have such a peaceful spirit. And I hope this story brings some peace to you.

Anndrena Belcher of Scott County, Virginia, has a master's degree in social sciences and worked in post-secondary education until 1981. A storyteller, singer, dancer, actress, and dress-up artist, she created a performing-arts project called For Old Times' Sake. Belcher has worked in public television and film, both commercial and documentary, and has written for teachers' guides and regional magazines.

THE CLEVER WIFE OF VIETNAM

Doug Lipman

Long ago in Vietnam there was a woman who lived, like many, in a small village, surrounded by her family. Every day she was greeted by her parents, grandparents, uncles, nieces, nephews, and cousins. She knew that when she married she wanted to live in a new family that was just as close as the family she would leave behind.

When she was old enough, she was courted by a man from another village who was famous there for his generosity to his many friends. She thought, *His charitable heart is just what I seek.*

But when she went to live with him, she found that his aged father was not given a place of honor at the dinner table. In fact, the old man was forced to sit in the corner and eat plain rice from a wooden bowl.

The new bride approached her husband courteously and said, "Perhaps your father would enjoy joining us."

The reply was gruff. "Him? Let him stay there. If you knew the things he did to me when I was young . . . " And she knew that—in that day and age—she was forbidden to bring up the matter a second time.

But that night she could not rest. Quietly she went to the old man and said, "Tomorrow before dinner, break your bowl."

"Break my bowl?" The old man's voice quivered. "He will make me eat with my bare hands!"

"I will take care of that. Break your bowl."

The next day at dinner she served her husband his delicious food in his beautiful ceramic bowl. Then she went to serve the old man. "Here is your plain rice," she said. "Give me your bowl."

The old man, too terrified to speak, merely held up the pieces of the broken bowl in his trembling hands. She said, "What? You have broken your bowl!"

The husband turned toward his father, and his eyes shone with anger.

The wife said, "You should not have broken your bowl. I was saving

When I first told this adapted Vietnamese folk tale about a triumphant woman, audiences thought the story was about her husband—until the very end. To establish her character earlier in the story, I added the incident of the broken bowl, which appears in several Asian variants. My version is recorded on Folktales of Strong Women *(Yellow Moon Press, 1983).*

it. When our sons are grown, I will need it for my husband."

At that moment the husband's eyes began to shine with a wholly different light. And with one silent gesture he motioned to the old man to join them at the table.

The young wife's dismay was not at an end, however. She soon learned that her husband's younger brother, who struggled to earn his living from a small, rocky farm, was not aided by his older brother.

In time she suggested to her husband, "Perhaps your younger brother would enjoy the generosity you give to your friends."

"That weakling?" he retorted. "If I give him help, how will he learn to stand on his own?"

Then one day the husband came home to find his wife very upset. "Oh, husband," she said, "a horrible thing has happened. A beggar came today, asking for food. I told him to wait in this room. When I came back with the food, he was taking one of our precious vases and putting it in his sack. I told him to put it back, but he wouldn't. I pushed him with my hands. Husband! I did not know my own strength. When I went to his limp body, I saw that his head had hit the sharp edge of the table and that he was dead.

"My first thought was, *The mandarin of this district is harsh in his judgments and will use this as an excuse to put us in prison.* So quickly I took the body and wrapped it in a rug in the other room. Husband, you must find some way to carry it into the woods and bury it under cover of darkness."

The husband was greatly disturbed and confused. "I'll ask one of my friends to help . . . That's what I'll do."

Right away he went off to his closest and dearest friend. "I'm so glad to see you," said the friend. "I was just about to have a game of cards. I'd love to have you join me. You always lose, sweet friend; do come in. But wait! I can see that you're troubled in some way. You can tell me. Go ahead."

The husband sighed with relief and told the whole story. "Oh yes," stammered the friend, "you'd like me to help you bury the body of someone you murdered today. Well . . . I'd be very happy to . . . Oh—I just remembered! My wife's mother is very sick. In fact, I was just on my way out the door to visit her. Please come back tomorrow."

Before the husband knew it, he was standing outside alone. In confusion and fear, he went straight to his next friend's house.

"How wonderful that you decided to pay me a call," said the friend. "I'm so pleased. There's just enough light left for a walk in the garden. Look at all these plants. Each one was provided by your beneficence. Wait! There's a shadow across your eyes—you have some kind of trouble. Please tell it to me. Whatever it is, I won't rest until it has been solved."

The husband thought, *At last, here is the friend I need*, and he told the entire story. "I see," the friend replied. "Of course, I'd be glad to help carry the—ooh!" The husband's friend held his side in pain. "Don't worry; it's just one of my attacks." He gasped, his face wrinkled in discomfort. "They get especially bad when I try to walk anywhere— gasp—or carry anything. Please come back another day."

Again the husband found himself alone, facing a closed door. He went to the house of his next friend. Even though he saw the glow of a fire inside, no one answered his knock. He went on to the next house and the next—the response was the same. Then he realized that his first two friends must have gone ahead to warn all the others. No one would open his door to him that night.

With rapid thoughts and slow steps, he returned home and told his wife what had happened.

"Husband," she said, "in that case, you must go ask your brother for help."

"Him? Why would he help me?"

"Husband, it's your only chance."

To his amazement, the husband found his brother surprised and concerned but most willing to help. Together the two of them carried two shovels and the wrapped body deep into the woods. Before daylight the two returned.

Hours later an imperious rapping at the door awakened the husband. It was the mandarin himself. The younger brother stood beside him, his captive, and behind him, gloating, were the two friends the husband had talked to the night before.

The mandarin's voice was like a cold wind. "You, sir, have had the impudence to commit a murder and not to report it to me immediately. Furthermore, you tried to entangle these two upstanding citizens in your web. Fortunately they had the good sense to report the matter to me immediately. Lead us to the evidence!"

The two friends led the way to the exact spot where the body was buried. The husband and brother now realized that they had been followed the night before.

"Yes," said the mandarin, "here is the mound of earth. Dig it up. We will have the trial and sentencing here and now."

The men removed the bundle and unrolled the rug. There before them they saw—the body of a large white dog! The mandarin looked at the friends, who looked at the brother, who looked at the husband, who looked at the wife.

She cast down her eyes and said, "Perhaps I should explain. For years I have wished my husband could understand the value of his brother's love, compared with the affection of those my husband calls his friends. Yesterday my dog died, and I saw my opportunity."

Immediately the mandarin understood what had happened. He whirled around to direct his scorn at the two informants. "You two call yourselves friends? You will be fined and whipped for being such false friends!"

As for the husband, wife, father, and brother, they lived until the end of their days in a family that was both close and warm.

Doug Lipman of West Somerville, Massachusetts, performs and leads storytelling workshops nationally. He specializes in the supportive coaching of storytellers and others who use oral communication. Lipman integrates music and audience participation into stories aimed at touching people deeply.

THE DAY IT SNOWED TORTILLAS

Joe Hayes

A third-grade girl at a school I visited told me about a woman who tricked her husband into believing it had rained buñuelos *(fried, sugar-sprinkled pastries). I was familiar with the tale from the collections of Juan B. Rael and other folklorists and decided to work out a telling of my own.*

This is the story of a poor woodcutter. He was good at his work. He could cut down a tree in no time, and he would split it into firewood and sell it in the village. He made a good living, but he wasn't well educated. He couldn't read or write. He wasn't very bright either. He was always doing foolish things, but he was lucky. He had a clever wife, and she would get him out of any trouble his foolishness got him into.

One day he was working far off in the mountains, and when he started home at day's end, he saw three leather bags by the side of the trail. He picked up the first bag and discovered that it was full of gold. He looked into the second. It was full of gold too. So was the third.

He loaded the bags onto his donkey and took them home to show his wife. She warned him, "Don't tell anyone you found this gold. It must belong to some robbers who have hidden it in the mountains. If they find out we have it, they'll kill us to get it back."

But then she thought, *Oh no! My husband can never keep a secret. What shall I do?* So she came up with a plan. She told her husband, "Before you do anything else, go to the village and get me a sack of flour. I need a big sack—100 pounds of flour."

The man went off to the village, grumbling to himself, "All day I work in the mountains, and now I have to drag home a hundred pounds of flour. I'm tired of all this work." But he bought the flour and took it home to his wife.

"Thank you," she told him. "You've worked awfully hard. Why don't you lie down and rest for a while?" He liked that idea. He lay down on the bed and soon fell fast asleep.

As soon as her husband started to snore, the woman went to work. She began to make tortillas. She made batch after batch. She made them until the stack reached clear up to the kitchen ceiling. She turned that whole hundred pounds of flour into tortillas. Then she took them outside and threw them all over the ground.

The woodcutter was so tired that he slept all evening and on through the night. He didn't wake up until the next morning. When he awoke, he stepped outside and saw that the ground was covered with tortillas. He called to his wife, "What's the meaning of this?"

His wife joined him at the door. "Oh my goodness! It must have snowed tortillas last night!"

"Snowed tortillas? I've never heard of such a thing."

"What? You've never heard of it snowing tortillas? You're not very well educated. You'd better go to school and learn something." So she packed him a lunch and made him go to school.

The woodcutter didn't know how to read or write so he was put into the first grade. He had to squeeze into one of the little chairs the children sat in. The teacher asked questions, and the children enthusiastically raised their hands. But the woodcutter didn't know the answers to any of those questions, and he grew more and more embarrassed. Finally he couldn't stand it any longer. He stomped out of the school and hurried home. Once he got there, he seized his ax and declared to his wife, "I've had enough education. I'm going to cut firewood."

"Fine," she called after him. "You go do your work."

About a week later the robbers showed up at the house, just as the woman had suspected they would. "Where's that gold your husband found?" they demanded.

The wife acted innocent. "Gold?" She shook her head. "I don't know anything about any gold."

"Come on!" the robbers said. "Your husband's been telling everyone in the village that he found three sacks of gold. They belong to us. You'd better give them back."

She looked disgusted. "Did my husband say that? Oh that man! He says the strangest things. I don't know anything about your gold."

"That's a likely story. We'll just wait here until he comes home and find out for ourselves." So the robbers waited around all day, passing the time sharpening their knives and cleaning their pistols. Toward evening the woodcutter came up the trail with his donkey. The robbers ran out and grabbed him roughly. "Where's that gold you found?"

The woodcutter scratched his head. "Gold?" he mumbled. "Oh yes. Now I remember. My wife hid it." He called out, "Wife, what did you do with that gold?"

His wife sounded puzzled. "What gold? I don't know what you're talking about."

"Sure you do. Don't you remember? The day before it snowed tortillas, I came home with three bags of gold. And in the morning you sent me to school."

The robbers looked at one another. "Did he say it snowed tortillas?" they whispered. "She sent him to school?" They shook their heads. "Why are we wasting our time with this numskull? He's out of his head!"

The robbers went away thinking the woodcutter was crazy and had just been talking a lot of nonsense, and they never came back. And from that day on, it didn't really matter whether the woodcutter was well educated or clever. It didn't even matter if he was a good woodcutter. He and his wife had three sacks of gold! They never could find out who the gold had really belonged to, so they had to keep it themselves.

Joe Hayes of Santa Fe, New Mexico, grew up in Arizona and was fascinated by tales of the American Southwest. He began his storytelling career by sharing those stories with his children, and in 1980 he became a professional teller.

BARNEY MCCABE

Guy Carawan

Once upon a time it was a twin sister and brother. The sister's name was Mary, and the brother's name was Jack. One day they decided to go on a long traveling. But Jack was a wise child, and he told Mary to go in the house and ask Mother could they go. Her mother say, "Yes, you can go, but take care."

Jack say, "Wait a minute, Sister," and went to the barn and got four grains of corn. Mary say to Jack, "What you gonna do with that corn?" Jack say, "You will see." So he put the corn in his pocket.

Before he left home, Jack told his mother, "Mama, I got three dogs—Barney McCabe, Doodle-le-doo, and Soo-boy. I'm going to leave a glass of milk on the table. If you see that glass of milk turn to blood, I want you to turn my dogs loose."

So they went on traveling and all the time wondering what was the end gonna be. Pretty soon it come dark, and they began to get weary. They knocked at an old lady's house. The old lady ran to the door, say, "Who is it?"

Jack say, "Me, Mama. Could we spend the night here? 'Cause we far from home, and we very tired." Old lady say, "Oh yes, come on in."

She was a witchcraft, and the children didn't know it. She fed them and put them to bed. She had a knife she call Tommy Hawk. After she put the children to bed, she began to sharpen it up.

Penny, get your knife,
Penny, get your knife,
Penny, get your knife; go shock 'em, shock 'em.

Hump back a Josie back, a see Antony,
Mama and your daddy tell me so.
See so, I think it so,
Tam-a-ram-a-ram.

I learned this story from Mrs. Janie Hunter on Johns Island, South Carolina, when I lived there in the early 1960s, and I've told it in concerts and festivals across the country ever since. These are Mrs. Hunter's words, though, and you can hear her tell the story in her African/ English Creole on the Smithsonian/ Folkways recording Been in the Storm So Long *(1990).*

Children say, "Grandma, what's all that noise? We can't sleep."

She say, "That ain't nothing but your grandma's frock-tail switchin' to get your supper hot. You all go back to sleep."

So Jack begin to wonder how they can get out of there. Then he remember the old lady have a room full of pumpkins. Jack take two pumpkins and put 'em in the bed and cover 'em over, pretend it was he and his sister.

Then Jack throw one grain of corn out the window, and it turn into a ladder. Jack and Mary climbed the ladder down, and they start traveling for home.

The old lady sharpen her knife faster:

Penny, get your knife,
Penny, get your knife,
Penny, get your knife; go shock 'em, shock 'em.

Hump back a Josie back, a see Antony,
Mama and your daddy tell me so.
See so, I think it so,
Tam-a-ram-a-ram.

She didn't hear no noise, so she sneak in the room and chop up the pumpkins in the bed. Then she ran in the kitchen and got a dishpan and pulled back the cover. And when she think she putting the meat in the pan to cook for breakfast, she drop the pumpkin in the pan. Jack and Mary was long gone.

She get mad, grab Tommy Hawk, and fly down on those children. The children drop another grain of corn, and it turn into a tall pine tree. And Jack and Mary flew up in that tree. The old lady start to cut on the tree, say:

A chip on the old block, a chip on the new block;
A chip on the old block, a chip on the new block.

Then Jack drop a grain of corn down from the pine tree, and back home that glass of milk turn to blood. Them dogs begin to holler. Jack's mother ran in the yard and turned the dogs loose. Jack say:

Barney McCabe and Doodle-le-doo and Soo-boy,
Your maussa almost gone.

Dogs say:

Maussa, Maussa, coming all the time;
Maussa, Maussa, coming all the time.

Old witch say:

A chip on the old block, a chip on the new block;
A chip on the old block, a chip on the new block.

Every time she chip, the tree lean and lean. Jack call:

Barney McCabe and Doodle-le-doo and Soo-boy,
Your maussa almost gone.

Dogs say:

Maussa, Maussa, coming all the time;
Maussa, Maussa, coming all the time.

Jack drop another corn—the last corn—and it turn into a bridge. When the old witch pull the ax up to take the last chop, and chop Jack and Mary in the head, the dogs ran up. Barney McCabe cut her throat, Doodle-le-doo suck her blood, and Soo-boy drag her on the bridge. The bridge bend, and that's the way that story end.

Based at the Highlander Center in New Market, Tennessee, Guy Carawan has performed throughout the United States, collecting and documenting regional culture and organizing cultural workshops along the way. His singing career spans 30 years, and his collecting efforts have resulted in a dozen documentary albums and four books.

HAYDN'S SONATA

Mara Capy

It was Israel, about 1980 or '81, the last night of our class in storytelling. I said, "Let's forget about techniques. Let's forget for a while about the hows and whys. It's our last evening together. Does anyone have a story to share—maybe some part of your life that you haven't shaped into a story yet or a story you would like to tell again?"

We rearranged the seats, drawing them into a circle. We shut down the lights and opened the curtains. The quiet glow of the ebbing sun filled the room. Somehow this ritual brought us together. We were no longer a class divided into teacher and students—we were just a group of people in a little room. And as our stories were shared, the room became smaller and smaller.

Then it was Hannah's turn to tell. She was a short dark woman with long straight hair and large dark eyes—the kind of eyes you could sink into and drown in if you let yourself go. She opened her eyes wide. Hesitant and shy, speaking in a thick voice, she began. "I've never told this before, but I'd like to tell it now.

"You know, all of us here in Israel have to go into training for the army—women as well as men. So that's how my story starts. I was stationed near Be'er Sheva', a small town fairly near the desert. The houses there are old, old houses once owned by rich Arab merchants. The stones are huge, laid one on top of another. They look as though they were gouged out of the earth's groin. High arches, high ceilings," she said, as she glanced upward.

"Well, I was stationed out there at the edge of the desert, and I had a weekend pass. I was very tired, and I was feeling so empty. What was this war all about? Was it ever going to end? It felt so purposeless. There wasn't time for me to go home for the Sabbath; Haifa was too far. My parents had given me the keys to one of the old houses in Be'er Sheva'. It was owned by some friends of theirs, and I was told I could use it whenever I had a weekend pass.

When the events of our lives are shaped into stories, they can touch others and create communication in ways beyond explanation. This story from the life of an Israeli woman deeply moved me. It captures the loneliness of war and the transcendent power of music and the human spirit.

"I took off in search of the house and soon found it. Pulling the keys from my pocket, I opened the heavy wooden door, and there before me was a very large room, mostly empty. There was an old table made of thick, thick wood, just as the house's doors were huge and thick— barriers against the world. There was a hand-carved metal knocker on the outside of the door. Flowering branches of bougainvillea, red and purple, hung in the window. They had once been well cared for.

"My eyes scanned the room, and in the corner—in the corner was a piano. A chill ran through my body. How much I loved music—how much I missed it. I took off my army jacket. I didn't bother to eat or look around. I closed the huge wooden door, pulled out the piano bench, blew the dust off the top of the piano, and touched it with love and gentleness. My fingers hit the keys, and I began to play. I played and played, and the music filled the room. I was almost in another world, far away from the war, from my duties, my loneliness.

"And then I began to play my favorite of favorites: Haydn's Sonata. As I played, I thought I heard a sound outside the house. I wasn't quite sure, but I was conscious of something, like tires on a sandy path coming to a stop. I continued to play the sonata, and when I finished, there was a clapping sound right outside the door.

"Someone was standing there, applauding my playing. I got up from the piano bench and moved toward the large wooden door. My hands almost touched it, but something held me back. I returned to the piano and sat down again and played until I was exhausted. Then I wrapped myself in a sheepskin and fell asleep.

"That was a long time ago," said Hannah. "The war, my piece of it, anyway, ended. I went back to Haifa, married, had a family, and eventually decided to do some volunteer work. Well, there are many homes for soldiers here, soldiers that have been hurt beyond repair. I would often go and play the piano for them. In one such home I struck up an acquaintance with a soldier whose face you could hardly see, it was so badly burned and scarred. We often spent time just talking.

"Well, one day I sat down at the piano, and my fingers found their way along the keys. He sat near me, and without thinking much about it, I started to play Haydn's Sonata. Tears began falling from his eyes. As I looked at him, he said, 'You know, once many years ago I was stationed near Be'er Sheva'. I was on leave for the weekend, and I was going home. The army van I was riding in stopped at a transfer point in front of an old Arab house. As I got off and waited to be picked up by the next transport vehicle going north, I heard music coming from the house. So I went to the front door and listened, and I heard my favorite song, Haydn's Sonata, coming from that old house.

"'I applauded,' he said, clapping his hands, 'because it touched me so, there in the desert in the middle of a war. I heard a shuffling sound inside and then nothing. I never knew who played that song. The truck came along, and I jumped in and went on my way. It meant a lot to me, though, that song.'

"I looked at him, and I didn't know what to do," Hannah said. "I was moved. I wondered, *Should I tell him?*"

"Well, Hannah?" We all moved forward in our seats. "Did you tell him?"

"No," she said, her dark eyes the kind you could sink into and drown in. "No. I couldn't—something inside stopped me."

Mara Capy of Brattleboro, Vermont, is a coordinator of dance/movement and expressive-arts-therapy students at Lesley College in Cambridge, Massachusetts. A story collector and writer, she has developed storytelling and healing programs for special-needs children, substance abusers, and cancer and AIDS patients.

THE OLD MAN WITH BIG EARS

Ephat Mujuru

In my native country of Zimbabwe, we accompany stories with the soft but lively sounds of the mbira (a hollow wooden instrument with metal strips that vibrate when plucked). I love to see people of all ages dancing while they listen to this ancient instrument. We believe that each mbira contains a spirit and is hence alive.

A long time ago, when this world was still very young, there lived an old, old man named Chamakanda. This old man lived in one of the villages in Africa, and he was a great friend of the children. All the children in that village loved to go to his house, and they would sing this song for him:

Chamakanda, Chamakanda . . .

Chamakanda was a great dancer, and whenever he heard that song, he would become very excited and dance for the children:

Dee, dee, dee . . .

The children loved to watch Chamakanda dance, and they would try to dance like he did:

Dee, dee, dee . . .

One day after Chamakanda had danced for a long time, he became tired. The children said, "Keep dancing; keep dancing." But Chamakanda said, "No, I must rest," and he sat down to rest by a tree. He fell deep asleep, and soon he started snoring. He snored so loud that the children could not stand to hear him, so they woke him up.

When he awoke, he was surprised that he had fallen asleep, and he quickly reached up to make sure he was still wearing his hat. Chamakanda always wore a very big old hat. No matter what he was doing, he always wore that hat. It was like a part of him. He wore it when he ate, when he slept, and even when he took his bath.

The children had noticed this hat, and they wondered why he always wore it. So on this day, when he woke up, one little boy asked him, "Chamakanda, why are you so worried about your old hat?" The child went straight up to him and tried to take the hat off. Chamakanda stopped him and said, "No, you can't do that. You're trying to do something that has never happened."

For three days and three nights after that, the child could not stop thinking about Chamakanda's hat. He was very curious. He really wanted to know the reason why Chamakanda always wore it, but nobody could tell him.

So he went back to Chamakanda with the idea of persuading him to take off his hat. First the child sang, and Chamakanda danced for a while. Then the boy began to ask Chamakanda, "Please, please, won't you take off your hat? I would like to see your head, even if it is a bald head. Are you not proud of your old age?"

Chamakanda said, "No, it's not that. Anyway, I don't want to talk about it."

But the child persisted. "Please, please, won't you take off your hat? I want to see your head."

Chamakanda was a very kind man, and he felt sorry for the child. So he thought for a while, and finally he said, "I will take off my hat on one condition: that you don't tell anyone what you are going to see."

The child promised him, saying, "I will not tell anyone. Not even my parents, not even my best friend."

Chamakanda took off his hat, and the child was amazed to see that Chamakanda had big hairy ears—just like a donkey's.

Then the child began to ask many questions because, of course, he wanted to know how Chamakanda got those enormous donkey's ears.

Chamakanda would not answer him. "I told you that I don't want to talk about it," he said.

So the child went on his way. Soon he saw his friend, and he said, "There is something that I am not going to tell you."

"What is it that you are not going to tell me?"

"I am not going to tell you that Chamakanda has got big ears that look like a donkey's," he said. Then he realized what he had done and begged his friend, "Oh, please don't tell anyone."

Well, that friend went and said to another friend, "I am not going to tell you that Chamakanda has got big ears that look like a donkey's. Don't tell anyone." That friend told another friend, and that one told another—and another and another.

This took place during the time when the trees used to talk, and the little boy was sitting under a tree, saying to himself, "I am not going to tell anyone that Chamakanda has got big ears that look like a donkey's."

By a strange coincidence, it happened that there was a great drummer in the village who wanted to make a new drum. So he went into the forest, and he chose the very same tree that the boy had been talking to. The man started chopping the tree, and when it fell down, he cut off the branches. Then he carved the trunk into a beautiful drum.

When he finished, he began to play his drum. But he was surprised to hear that his drum was singing with a human voice:

Ka dan dan da dan
Don't tell anyone
Ka dan, ka dan
That Chamakanda has got big ears
Ka dan dan da dan
That look like a donkey's.

The drummer was very happy with the sound of his new drum, and he wanted other people to hear it too. He went all around the village saying, "You must come and hear this amazing drum." And when people heard the sound of the drum, it was so magnificent that they became convinced that the news about Chamakanda's ears must be true.

Soon it was the story of the entire village. The people were saying it. The trees were saying it. Even the wind was whistling, "Chamakanda has got big ears that look like a donkey's. Please, don't tell anyone."

By then thousands and thousands of people had heard about Chamakanda's ears. One morning they decided to go to his house and see for themselves. The children led the way, singing:

Chamakanda, Chamakanda . . .

Chamakanda heard the people singing. When he realized they were singing about his ears, he was astonished. Then he saw the people coming toward his house, and he ran away.

When the people arrived at his house, they found the door open, but Chamakanda was not there. The children were very upset. They began calling, "Chamakanda! Come back. We want to see your ears. We aren't going to tell anyone."

Chamakanda did not answer. The people looked for him everywhere for many days, but they could not find him. Even today they are still looking for Chamakanda.

So the moral of the story is that you should never, never tell anyone what you are told not to tell.

Ephat Mujuru, a Shona mbira master, comes from a family known for many generations for storytelling and mbira playing. When he's not traveling the world to "bring mbira to the people," he teaches at the College of Music in Harare, Zimbabwe. Mujuru has appeared in many countries, on television and radio and in concert, and he particularly loves giving workshops and concerts for children.

MEDUSA

Barbara McBride-Smith

You've heard of Dracula and Frankenstein and Godzilla and the Swamp Thing. Now I'd like to tell you the story of the most horrifying, the most terrifying, the most god-awful monster of them all. She was known to the ancient Greeks as Medusa.

Did you ever hear the sad story of Medusa? She was the ugliest woman who ever lived. Why, she was so ugly—she was so-o-o ugly—if you looked her right in the face, you'd turn to stone.

Yes indeed, hers was a real sad story. You see, she hadn't always been ugly. She started out with the looks of a goddess, so naturally she attracted lots of gods. But she got herself involved in one too many dangerous liaisons, if you know what I mean. The last one was a fatal attraction, and it was with Poseidon.

You've heard of Poseidon, the god of the sea, the one who ran around with a pitchfork in his hand and seaweed in his hair and his participles a-dangling. Poseidon and Medusa rendezvoused one night in the nearest empty building they could find. Unfortunately, it turned out to be a temple of the goddess Athena, and when Athena heard about it, she was furious.

Athena was the leader of the Mount Olympus Moral Majority. She was always trying to improve the standards up there, trying to keep the neighborhood from going downhill. She was also chief of the Evelyn Wood School of Speed Revenge. Well, somebody had to be punished for defiling her temple.

Now, Poseidon had connections—he was Zeus's brother. Athena couldn't touch him. But Medusa had no connections at all, so she had to bear the brunt of Athena's wrath. Athena knew just how to hurt a woman right smart. She took away Medusa's beauty—all of it—and made her the ugliest woman who had ever lived.

Did you ask me how ugly she was? They say she had bulging, glaring eyes, enormous teeth that looked like fangs, and a huge tongue that hung out of her mouth like she'd been French-kissing for a week. Her breath smelled like a dog had died in her mouth.

And her hair! It wasn't just stringy. Athena gave her snakes for hair—dozens of self-willed little strands, each one of them curling and coiling and hissing and going its own way. She couldn't do a thing with that hair. She tried everything—mousse, gel, curling irons, perms. Nothing worked!

As for the rest of her body, Athena gave her hard scaly skin like a lizard, wings like a bat, and claws like a vulture. She was a terrible sight.

But the worst part was what her new ugliness did to her social life. Oh, at first there was a brief period when she was something of a celebrity. Stories about her were splashed across the front page of the *National Enquirer.* You'd hear people in line at the grocery store say, "Wooee, look at that! The ugliest woman in the world! Yessir, I want to see her in the flesh, if it's the last thing I do." And if they did, it was.

Because nobody could look directly at her and live to tell about it. One glance and you'd turn to stone. So of course, nobody wanted to have her around. Here she was, the original party girl, and now she couldn't draw flies at a picnic.

There was nothing for her to do but leave her old neighborhood and go off to some desolate place where nobody would have to look at her. The gods allowed her two unattractive spinster sisters to go along with her for company. The three of them found a desert island and planned to spend the rest of their miserable days there.

Now, right about here in a story like this, you usually hear about a handsome young man—a prince, maybe—who chances upon a hapless maiden and changes her life. Well, this story does have a handsome young man, a hero, in fact. He chanced upon Medusa and changed her life. The fact is, she lost her head over him.

The name of this hero was Perseus. He began life not as a mere mortal but as the son of Zeus. That meant he was only semimortal, and he was fated to do great things.

Perseus was born under unusual circumstances. His mother,

Danae, was a princess who'd had a falling out with her daddy, the king. It seems as how the king had a habit of visiting a place called Delphi to seek the advice of a fortuneteller called an oracle. Why he wasn't satisfied with relying on his horoscope like any normal head of state is a mystery to me. Anyway, this oracle told him that the son of his daughter—his own grandson—would kill him someday.

As soon as the king got home, he locked his daughter, Danae, up in a tower and forbade anyone, especially any man, to visit her. That way, she could never have a child.

Right? Wrong! Because the king didn't count on Zeus, who never could resist a damsel in distress—or a damsel of any kind, for that matter. So Danae got struck by Zeus's power. Later she said it felt like a bolt of lightning. And then she gave birth to a son. She named him Perseus, which means "the avenger."

Now her daddy, the king, had to fall back on Plan B. He figured out that this hadn't been a normal birth, so he had to be careful how he handled things. He couldn't just kill the baby. So he locked the mother and child in a wooden trunk and threw them in the ocean. If they suffocated or drowned, it wasn't exactly his fault, was it?

But the gods were with Danae and Perseus, and the trunk was washed up safe on a distant shore. An old fisherman found them, took them in, and cared for them. And so it was that Perseus, the son of a god and the grandson of a king, grew up in a humble fisherman's shack. But his mother told him he was going to be a hero someday, and his first opportunity came just about the time most boys get their driver's license.

The king of this new land where they lived was named Polydectes. He decided he wanted to marry Perseus' mother. But Polydectes was an evil dirt bag, and Danae didn't want to marry him. So Perseus went to Polydectes's bachelor party and promised to give him any present he wanted if he wouldn't force Danae to marry him.

King Polydectes was delighted. Here was his chance to get rid of Danae's snotty-nosed kid. "You're on, boy!" said King Polydectes. "Bring me the head of Medusa."

I told you Perseus was a hero, right? The gods have a way of watching over their heroes. In this case, it was Athena whose ears perked up as soon as she heard the name *Medusa*. She was still ticked off at Medusa for defiling her temple, and she couldn't pass up another opportunity to get even with her. Athena decided to give Perseus all the help she could.

Athena sent Hermes, the messenger of the gods, down to outfit Perseus for his quest. Hermes explained to Perseus that this was a special mission and that it would require some special equipment. He took Perseus to the Mount Olympus laboratories and outfitted him in the latest high-tech adventure gear. He gave him wing-tipped sandals so he could fly, a helmet that would make him invisible, and a special sword that could cut through steel. Then Hermes gave Perseus a shield with a finish so bright that it reflected images like a mirror. He explained that this would protect him from the power of Medusa, because if he looked at her reflection and not straight at her, he wouldn't be turned to stone. Finally Hermes gave Perseus a matching handbag. But it was a magic handbag, powerful enough to hold the bloody head of Medusa. And all of that for only $29.95 plus tax!

Perseus buckled on his wing-tipped sandals and flew to the desert island where Medusa lived. He followed a trail of stone sightseers until he came to an old run-down castle. He knew Medusa must be inside because he saw tongue tracks going up the steps.

It wasn't easy walking in backwards while looking in a mirror, but somehow he managed. Then he saw her reflection. Wooee! She was even uglier than he had imagined. She looked like something that would crawl up under the refrigerator when the kitchen light's turned on. He asked himself, "How come I had to get the adventure with the ugly woman in it?"

Luckily for him, Medusa was asleep. So he crept up on her, still looking in the mirror, waited until he got in just the right position, raised his sword, and—*ka-chunk*—chopped off her head. Mercy, what a mess! He had to feel back behind him and find that writhing head of snakes and put it in his magic handbag. Then he put on his helmet of invisibility so Medusa's sisters couldn't see him, and he was outta there.

When Perseus got back home, he discovered that that slime-ball King Polydectes had already reneged on their deal. Polydectes had convinced Danae that Perseus was dead and that she had to live up to their contract by marrying him. Perseus arrived back in town just as the prenuptial celebration was beginning.

When Polydectes saw Perseus standing in the doorway of his officers' quarters, he ordered all his soldiers to take aim at the boy and fire on command. But Perseus still had one more trick in his bag. Perseus said just what my teenage son would say: "Go ahead, butt-face, make my day!" Of course, he said it in Greek. Then he whipped out the head of Medusa and held it high in the air, and Polydectes and all his soldiers were turned to stone.

Right away the common folks in the kingdom elected Perseus as their new king. Perseus said thanks anyway, but he'd rather be a full-time professional hero. So he turned the kingship over to the old fisherman who had been like a father to him.

Danae told Perseus he deserved a little vacation after all he'd been through. So the two of them took a cruise—one of those five-day, four-night deals—and ended up in the same country where Perseus had been born. A big track meet was being held at one of the seaside resorts, and since the organizers recognized Perseus as a hero, they invited him to enter the event of his choice. Perseus had inherited his father's skill at throwing things—you remember how Zeus loved to throw bolts of thunder and lightning—so Perseus entered the discus throw.

Now, either Perseus lost control, or the wind caught the discus—nobody ever knew for sure—but it sailed into the grandstand and hit an old man right upside the head. It killed him instantly. Perseus reached the old guy at the same time his mother did. Danae uttered just one word: "Daddy!"

And so the old prophecy of the oracle at Delphi came true. Perseus killed his own grandfather.

And what about Medusa? Well, that poor girl never did manage to pull herself back together. The best you can say for her is that her whole body was recycled. Athena used Medusa's head to decorate her shield. Her skin was used to make chastity belts for an entire army of Amazons. And her blood was used as an antidote for right-wing fundamentalism.

Maybe it's true what they say: Beauty is only skin-deep, but ugly goes clear to the bone.

Barbara McBride-Smith of Stillwater, Oklahoma, is a storyteller, librarian, comedian, and historian. She also teaches homiletics at Phillips Graduate Seminary. Known for her humorous interpretations of the Greek myths, the Texas-born teller notes that her characters are magnifications of her fellow Texans.

MARY AND THE SEAL

Duncan Williamson

Many years ago on a little isle off the west coast of Scotland—it could be Mull, Tiree, or any island—there lived an old fisherman and his wife. The old fisherman spent his entire life fishing in the sea and selling whatever fish he couldn't use himself to keep him and his wife and his little daughter alive.

They lived in a little cottage by the sea, and not far from where they stayed was the village, a very small village—just a post office, a hall, and some cottages. Everyone knew everyone else. His cousin also had a house in the village.

This old man and woman had a daughter called Mary, and they loved her dearly. She was such a nice child. She helped her father with the fishing, and when she was finished helping her father, she always came and helped her mother do housework and everything else.

The father used to set his nets every day in the sea, and he used to rise early every morning. Mary would get up and help her father lift his nets and collect the fish. After that was done, she'd help her mother, then go off to school. Everybody was happy for Mary, and her father and mother were so proud of her because she was such a good worker. She was a quiet and tender little girl and paid no attention to anyone outside the family. Well, the years passed by, and Mary grew till she became a young teenager.

That's where this story really begins, when Mary was about 16 or 17. She used to borrow her father's boat every evening in the summertime and go for a sail to an island that lay about half a mile from where they stayed, a little island out in the middle of the sea-loch. Mary used to spend all her spare time on the island.

When she'd finished her day's work with her father and helped her mother and had her supper, she would say, "Father, can I borrow your boat?" Even in the winter sometimes, when the sea wasn't too rough, she'd go out there and spend her time. Her father and mother never paid any attention because Mary's spare time was her own—when her work was finished, she could do what she liked. Till one day.

Her mother used to walk down to the small village and to the post office, where they bought their small quantity of messages and did their shopping. It was the only place they could buy any supplies. She heard two old women nattering to each other. Mary's mother's back was turned at the time, but she overheard the two old women. They were busy talking about Mary.

"Och," one woman said, "she's such a nice girl, but she's so quiet. She doesn't come to any of the dances; she doesn't even have a boyfriend. She doesn't do anything—we have our ceilidhs [song and story get-togethers] and things, but we never see her come; she never even pays us a visit. Such a nice quiet girl, but all she wants to do, she tells me, is take her boat and row over to the island and spend all her time there. Never even comes and has a wee timey [visit with someone]. And her mother and father are such decent people . . . even her Uncle Lachy gets upset."

This was the first time her mother had heard these whispers, so she paid little attention. She came home, and she was a wee bit upset. The next time she went back to the village, she heard the same whispers again, and this began to get into her mind—she began to think. But otherwise Mary was just a natural girl; she helped her daddy and she asked her mummy if there was anything she could do, helped her to do everything in the house, and she was natural in every way. But she kept herself to herself.

One evening it was suppertime once more, and after supper Mary said, "Daddy, can I borrow your boat?"

"Oh yes, Mary, my dear," he said, "you can borrow the boat. I'm sure I'm finished—we've finished our day's work. You can have the boat." It wasn't far across to row the little boat, maybe several hundred yards to the wee island in the loch. The old woman and the old man sat by the fire.

Once Mary had walked out the door and said goodbye to her father and mother, the old woman turned round and said to her husband, "There she goes again. That's her gone again."

Mary's father turned round and said, "What do you mean, Margaret? You know Mary always goes off and enjoys herself in the boat."

She said, "Angus, you don't know what I mean; it's not you that has got to go down to the village and listen to the whispers of the people and the talk and the wagging tongues."

He said, "Woman, what are you talking about?"

She said, "I'm talking about your daughter."

Angus didn't know what to say. He said, "What's wrong with my daughter? I'm sure she works hard, and she deserves a little time by herself. What's the trouble? Was there something you needed done that she didn't do?"

"Not at all," she said. "That's not what I'm talking about."

"Well," he said, "tell me what you're trying to say!"

She said, "Angus, it's Mary—the people in the village are beginning to talk."

"And what are they saying," he said, "about my daughter?" And he started to get angry.

"They're talking about Mary going off by herself in her boat to the island and spending all her time there. She's done that now for close on five years. And they say she doesn't go to any dances, she doesn't go to any parties, she doesn't accept any invitations to go anywhere, and she has no boyfriend. The wagging tongues in the village are talking about this. It's getting through to me, and I just don't like it."

"Well," he said, "Mother, I'm sure there's nothing in the world that should upset you about that; I'm sure Mary's minding her own business. And if she's out there, she's no skylarking with some young man— would you rather have her skylarking around the village with some young man or something? And destroying herself and bringing back a baby to you—would you enjoy that better?"

"It's not that, Angus," she said, "it's just that Mary is so unsociable."

Anyway, they argued and bargued for about an hour, and they couldn't get any further. About the time they were finished, Mary came in again. She was so radiant and happy.

She came over, kissed her mother and her daddy, and said, "Daddy, I pulled the boat up on the beach, and everything's all right."

He said, "All right, Daughter, that's nice."

"And," she said, "Daddy, the tide is coming in, and some of the corks of the net are nearly sunk, so I think we'll have a good fishing in the morning. I'll be up bright and early to give you a hand."

He said, "Thank you, Mary, very much."

She kissed her mother and said, "I'll just have a small something to eat, and I'll go to bed."

The old woman was still unsettled. "There she goes again," she said. "That's all we get."

"Well," he said, "what more do you expect? She's doing her best, Mother. She's enjoying herself."

"What is she doing on that island? That's what I want to know."

Said the old man to Margaret, "Well, she's no doing any harm out there."

The next morning they were up bright and early and had their breakfast. Mary went out with her father, collected the nets, and collected the fish, and they graded the fish and kept some for themselves. Then they went into the village and sold the rest, came back home, had their supper. It was a beautiful day.

Mary said, "Is there anything you want me to do, Mother?"

"Well, no, Mary," she said, "everything is properly done; the washing's finished and the cleaning's finished, and I was just making some jam. I'm sure your father's going to sit down and have a rest because he's had a hard day."

Mary turned round, and she said, "Father, could I borrow your boat?" once again.

"I'm sure, my dear," he said, "you can have the boat. Now, be careful because there might be a rise of a storm."

"I'll be all right, Father," she said. "I don't think it's going to—the sky looks so quiet and peaceful. I doubt if we'll have a storm tonight." And away she went.

As soon as she took off in the boat, oh, her mother got up. "That's it; there she goes again," she said. "To put my mind at rest, would you do something for me?"

Angus said, "What is it you want now, woman?"

"Look," she said, "would you relieve my mind for me? Would you go down and borrow your cousin Lachy's boat and row out to the island and see what Mary does when she goes there? It'll put my mind at rest."

"That's no reason for me to go out," he said. "Let the lassie enjoy herself if she wants to enjoy herself. There's no reason for me to go out—I'm sure there's no one within miles. Maybe she's wading on the beach and she sits there, and maybe she has some books with her, and she—she likes to be by herself."

But no. She said, "Look, do something for me, Husband! Would you go out, Angus, and see what she does?"

Angus said, "Och, dash it, woman! To keep you happy, I'll go out and see what she's doing. It's only a waste of time anyway."

So he walked down; it was only about 200 yards to Lachy's cottage.

Lachy had the same kind of boat. He was sitting at the fire. He had never married; their fathers had been brothers. Lachy was an old retired seaman, and he always liked to keep a boat.

"Well, it's yourself, Angus!" he said. "Come away in, sit down, and we'll have a wee dram."

"No," he said, "Lachy, I'm not here for a dram."

"Well," he said, "what sent you down? It's not often you come for a visit."

"I was wondering," he said, "if you would let me borrow your boat for a few minutes."

Lachy said, "Well, what's the trouble?"

"Ach, it's not trouble, really," he said. "I was just wanting to borrow your boat for maybe half an hour or so."

"Well, what is wrong with your own boat?"

"Och," he said, "Mary's using it."

Lachy said, "Och, that's Mary off on her gallivant to the island again. And you want to follow the lassie and see what she's doing. If I were you, I would leave her alone. Come on, sit down, and have a dram with me, and forget about it."

But old Angus was so persistent: "I want to borrow your boat."

"Well," he said, "take the dashit thing, and away you go!"

He took the boat and rowed across to the island and landed on the small beach. There was Mary's boat. He pulled his cousin Lachy's boat up beside Mary's and beached it, and he walked up the path—it was well-worn because Mary had walked up it many, many times. He followed the path up and went over a little knowe [hillock]. There were some rocks and a few trees, and down at the back of the island was a small kind of valley-shaped place that led out to the sea. Then there was a beach, and on the beach was a large rock. Beside the rock was a wee green patch.

Old Angus came walking up, taking his time—looked all around. There were a few seagulls flying around and a few birds wading along the beach because the tide was on the ebb. And he heard laughter coming on. Giggling and laughing—that was Mary, carrying on. He came up over the knowe, he looked down, and there was Mary—with a large gray seal. They were having the greatest fun you've ever seen. They were wrestling in the sand, carrying on and laughing. The seal was grunting, and Mary was flinging her arms around the seal!

Angus stopped, and he sat down and watched for a wee while. He said, "Ach, I'm sure she's doing no harm; it's only a seal. And her mother was so worried about it. She's enjoying herself; probably she's reared it up from a pup, and she comes over to feed it, and I'm sure it won't do her any harm. She's better playing with a seal than carrying on with a young bachal [wild young man] as far as I'm concerned."

He took his boat and rowed home, gave his cousin Lachy back the boat, lit his pipe, and walked up to his own home. He came in through the door, and his old wife, old Margaret, was waiting on him.

She said, "You're home, Angus."

"Aye, I'm home," he said. "Margaret, I'm home. And thanks be praised to God I am home."

She said, "Did you see Mary?"

"Of course," he said, "I saw Mary. She's out on the island."

"And what is she doing? Is she sitting—what is she doing?"

He said, "She's enjoying herself."

Old Margaret said, "What way is she enjoying herself—is she wading on the beach?"

"No," he said, "she's not wading on the beach."

"Is she reading?"

"No, she's not reading," he said. "She's playing herself with a seal."

She said, "What did you say?"

He said, "She's playing herself—she has the best company in the world, and she's enjoying herself. She's playing with a seal. A large gray seal. They're having great fun, and I didn't interfere."

She said, "Angus, Mary's enchanted. It's one of the sea-people that's taken over. Your daughter is finished—ruined forevermore. I've heard stories from my grandmother how the sea-people take over a person and take them away forevermore; they're never seen again. She's enchanted. What kind of a seal was it?"

He said, "It was a gray seal, and they were having good fun, so I didn't interfere."

She said, "If you want to protect your daughter and you want to have your daughter for any length of time, you'd better get rid of the seal."

He said, "Margaret, I couldn't interfere with them. It's Mary's pet."

"I don't care if it's Mary's pet or no," she said. "Tomorrow morning you will take your gun and go out. Instead of going to the fish, you'll go out, and you'll shoot that seal and destroy it forevermore!"

"But," he said, "it's Mary's pet—she probably reared it up unknown to us from a young pup, and it's not for me to destroy the seal, the thing she has to play with."

"I'm sure she can find plenty of company in the village instead of going out there to the island!"

Well, the argument went on, and they argued and bargued, and finally old Margaret won. Angus lit his pipe to have a smoke before going to bed.

"Well," he said, "in the morning I'll go out and see."

Then Mary came home, and she was so radiant and so bright, so happy. She came in and kissed her daddy and kissed her mummy. She had a cup of tea and asked Mummy and Daddy if they needed anything or wanted anything done.

They said, "No, Mary."

The old woman was a wee bit dubious. She wasn't just a wee bit too pleased, and Mary saw this.

She said, "Is there something wrong, Mother?"

"No, Mary," she said, "there's nothing wrong."

"Well, I'm going off to my bed." Mary went to her bed. In those cottages in times long ago in the little crofts, the elderly people stayed down on the floor, and there was a small ladder that led up to the garret in the roof. If people had any children, they had their beds in the garret. Mary lived upstairs.

The next morning Angus got up early, and before he even had any breakfast, he went into the back of the house and took his gun. He loaded it and took his boat, and he rowed out to the island before Mary was up. He walked up the path, the way Mary usually went, over the little hillock, down the little path to the little green patch beside the bare rock—and sure enough, sitting there, sunning himself in the morning sun was the seal.

Angus crept up as close as he could—and he fired a shot at the seal, hit the seal. The seal reared up, fell, and then crawled, hobbled its way into the sea and disappeared. "That's got you," he said.

And then he felt queer. A funny sensation came over him, and he sat down. He felt so funny—as though he had shot his wife or his daughter. A sadness came over him. He sat for a long while, and he looked at the gun. He felt that he had done something terrible. He felt so queer.

Then he picked up the gun and walked back to his boat, and he could barely walk, he felt so sick. He put the gun in the boat. He sat for a while before he could even take off in the boat, and he had the queer sensation—a feeling of loss was within him, a terrible feeling of loss— that something he had done could never be undone. He could hardly row the boat. But he finally made his way back to the mainland, tied up his boat, picked up the gun, and put it back in the cupboard. He walked in, and old Margaret was sitting there.

She said, "You're back, Angus."

He said, "Yes, I'm back."

She said, "Did you do what I told you to do?"

"Yes, Mother," he said, "I did what you told me to do."

She said, "Did you see the seal?"

"Yes," he said, "I saw the seal. And I shot the seal."

She sat down. "Are you wanting . . . "

"No, I don't want any breakfast," he said.

She said, "Are you feeling . . . "

"No, I'm not feeling very well; I'm not feeling very well at all."

She said, "What's wrong with you?"

"Well," he said, "I feel terrible, I feel queer, and I feel so kind of sad. I've done something wrong, and you forced me to it. I hope in the future that you'll be sorry for it."

"Och," she said, "it's only a seal."

But they said no more. By this time Mary had come down.

She said, "Good morning, Father; good morning, Mother," and she sat down at the table as radiant as a flower and had some breakfast. "Are you not eating, Daddy?"

"No," he said, "Daughter, I don't . . . "

She said, "Are you not feeling very well?" And she came over and stroked her father's head. "Are you not feeling very well, Father?"

"Oh," he said, "I'm feeling fine, Mary. I'm just not what I should be."

The mother tried to hide her face in case Mary could see a giveaway in her expression.

"Well," she said, "Father, are you ready to go out to lift the net?"

"Well, Mary, to tell you the truth," he said, "I don't think the outgoing tide will be for a while yet. No, I think I'll sit here and have a smoke."

"Mother," she said, "are you needing anything done?"

"No, Mary," she said, "we don't need anything done."

Now, they wanted to try to be as canny with her as possible. They didn't want to upset her in any way.

The mother said, "No, Mary, I think everything's done. There's only a little cleaning to be done, and I think I'll manage."

Mary said, "Well, after I milk the cow, Father, would it be all right if I take the boat?"

"Och, yes, Daughter, go ahead and help yourself to the boat," he said. "I'm sure you can have the boat anytime. You don't need to ask me for the boat; just take it whenever you feel like it."

So Mary milked the cow, brought in the milk, set the basins for the cream, and did everything that was needing to be done. Then she said, "Goodbye, Mother; I'm just going off for a while to be by myself—I'll be back before very long."

Mother said, "There she goes again. If you tell me it's true, she'll be home sadder and wiser."

Old Angus never said a word. He just sat and smoked his pipe, and he still had this feeling—as if a lump were in his heart. He was under deep depression; just didn't want to get up, just wanted to sit. He had this great terrible feeling of loss.

So Mary rowed the boat over to the island. Angus sat by the fire, and he smoked, and he smoked, and he smoked. Maggie called him for dinner, and the day passed by, but Mary never returned. Evening meal came; Mary never returned. Her mother began to get worried.

She came down and said, "Angus, has Mary come home? It'll soon be time for milking the cow again."

"No," he said, "Mary has never come."

"Would you go down and see if the boat's in?" she said. "Maybe she walked down to the village."

Angus went out, and there was no sign of the boat. "No," he said, "the boat . . . "

"Well, she's not home. If the boat's not home, she's not home," she said. "I doubt [fear] something's happened to her. Angus, you'll have to go and see what; you'll have to go out to the island. Go down and get Lachy's boat, and go out to the island and see."

Angus walked down and took Lachy's boat—never asked permission, just pulled the rope, untied the rope, and jumped in the boat. He didn't even worry about what would happen, he was so upset.

He rowed out to the island, and there was Mary's boat. He pulled Lachy's boat in because the beach was quite shallow, and he lay the boat beside Mary's boat, his own boat. He walked up the path, over the little hillock, down the big rock to the little bay and the green patch beside the rock and walked right down to where he had seen the seal. He looked. The side of the rock was splattered with blood where he had shot the seal. He walked round the whole island, which wasn't very big, walked the whole island round—and all he saw was a few spots of blood.

Nowhere did he find Mary. She had completely disappeared. There wasn't a sign of her, not even a footprint. He walked round once, he walked round twice, and he went round a third time. Every tree, every bush, every rock he searched, but Mary was gone.

He felt so sad. "What could happen to Mary, my poor wee Mary, what happened to her?"

Then at the very last he came back once again to the rock where he had shot the seal, and he looked out to sea. The tide was on the ebb. He stood and looked for a long, long while. He looked at the rock and saw that the blood was drying in the sun. He looked again, and then—all in a moment—up came two seals, two gray seals, and they came right out of the water, barely more than 25 yards from where he stood.

They looked at him—directly at him—then disappeared back down into the water. And he had a queer feeling that he was never going to see Mary anymore.

He took his boat, and he rowed home and tied it up. Just the one boat; he left Lachy's boat on the island. He sat down beside the fire. His wife, Margaret, came to him.

She said, "Did you see Mary?"

"No," he said, "I never saw Mary. I never saw Mary, I searched the entire island for Mary, and Mary is gone. And look, between you and me, she's gone forever. We'll never see Mary again."

They waited, and they waited; they waited for the entire days of their lives, but Mary never returned.

Duncan Williamson of Fife, Scotland, was born in a tinker's tent on the shores of Loch Fyne in 1928. He grew up in a family of traveling singers, pipers, and raconteurs and has been called "the national monument of British storytelling." Williamson continues to collect, publish, and perform the stories of his homeland.

The Lion and the Elephant

Alice McGill

Who is the king of the animals? The lion, you say?

It's true that when a lion puts his mouth to the ground and roars, his voice is so deep and so big and so heavy that it can be heard five miles away. But once long ago an especially big lion put his mouth to the ground and roared, and his voice was so big and so deep and so heavy that it could be heard 10 miles away.

When the other animals heard his voice rippling through the trees and rumbling through the dirt, they screamed and hollered, "Get out of the way! Run for your lives! It's the voice of the lion!" Some even fell out of the trees in a dead faint, they were so scared.

The lion saw them all running and screaming and fainting and having heart attacks right there before him, and he said to himself, "Whew, I must be powerful! Look at them all running away from me." He said, "I bet I could be king of this place if I wanted to be."

The more he thought about it, the more he wanted to be king—and the more he wanted somebody to tell him he was king. You see, you can't really be king unless somebody says you are.

So he went walking, looking for somebody to tell him he was king of the animals. Well, as you know, everyone had run away. He had to walk more than two hours before he spotted a great big zebra in the tall grass. The lion called the zebra to him: "Hey, stripes! Get over here!"

Zebra jumped out of that tall grass and went running right up to the lion. "Yes, sir, Mr. Lion," he said, "what can I do for you today?"

Lion said, "I want you to answer a question."

Zebra said, "What is it, sir?"

Lion said, "I want you to tell me who is the king of the beasts."

Zebra said, "You are, Mr. Lion. You're the king of the beasts, sir."

"Good," said the lion. "Now get away from me." Zebra took off so fast that he left some of his stripes behind, hanging on the tall grass.

The lion went on, strutting and roaring at will. He walked another

All my life I've heard that the male lion was king of the jungle and that his voice could make the very ground tremble. I think that the jury's still out about whether he's truly the king. This story about two animals, the lion and the elephant, proves that actions speak louder than words, or "It's better to say 'Yonder he goes' than 'There he lay.'"

123

hour and then eased up on a leopard lying fast asleep on a dead limb. The lion stood over him as he said, "Spots! Get up from there!" He went over the same little tale with the leopard, and the leopard, of course, said, "You're the king, sir. You're the king of the animals."

"Good," said the lion. "Now get away from me."

Well, the lion went on, strutting and roaring at will. Finally around sundown he spotted a great big she-elephant standing under a huge tree. So he called to her, "Hey, trunks!"

She took her time, walked straight up to him, and said, "Did you call me?"

He said, "Yes, I called you."

She said, "What do you want?"

He said, "I want to ask you a question. Who is the king of the beasts?"

Well, the elephant smiled. She reached out her trunk like she was going to give him a great big hug, and she wrapped it around his neck. Then she spun him up in the air! Twirled him around! Plopped him on the ground and kicked him from here to there.

The lion got up when she started for him again and said, "Wait a minute, woman, stop! You don't have to act like that just because you don't know the answer!"

Who is the king of the animals? Don't you answer that.

But folks tell me an elephant and a lion never drink from a watering hole at the same time. That's all there is to it.

Alice McGill was born and reared in North Carolina and now lives in Columbia, Maryland. She has a master's degree in education and taught school for many years before becoming a professional storyteller. The award-winning McGill's work has been featured in National Geographic's Storytelling in North America series.

GLUSCABI AND THE WIND EAGLE

Joseph Bruchac

Long ago Gluscabi lived with his grandmother, Woodchuck, in a small lodge beside the big water. One day when Gluscabi was walking around, he looked over and saw some ducks in the bay.

"I think it is time to go hunt some ducks," he said. So he took his bow and arrows and got into his canoe. He began to paddle out into the bay, and as he paddled, he sang:

> *Ki yo wah ji neh*
> *Yo hey ho hey*
> *Ki yo wah ji neh*
> *Ki yo wah ji neh.*

But a wind came up, and it turned his canoe and blew him back to shore. Once again Gluscabi began to paddle out, and this time he sang his song a little harder:

> *Ki yo wah ji neh*
> *Yo hey ho hey*
> *Ki yo wah ji neh*
> *Ki yo wah ji neh.*

Once again the wind came and blew him back to shore. Four times he tried to paddle out into the bay, and four times he failed. He was not happy. He went back to the lodge of his grandmother and walked right in, even though there was a stick leaning across the door, which meant that the person inside was doing some work and did not want to be disturbed.

"Grandmother," Gluscabi said, "What makes the wind blow?"

Grandmother Woodchuck looked up from her work. "Gluscabi," she said, "why do you want to know?"

Gluscabi is the hero of many stories of the Abenaki people, whose traditional homelands are the northeast corner of this continent. The best stories are those that entertain and teach, and this tale offers lessons about the wisdom of elders and the power and balance of the natural world—a world that too many people think they can completely control.

Then Gluscabi answered her just as all children do when they are asked such a question. "Because," he said.

Grandmother Woodchuck looked at him. "Ah, Gluscabi," she said, "whenever you ask such questions, I feel there is going to be trouble. Perhaps I should not tell you. But I know that you are so stubborn that you will never stop asking until I answer you. So I shall tell you. Far from here, on top of the tallest mountain, a great bird stands. This bird is named Wuchowsen, and when he flaps his wings, he makes the wind blow."

"Eh-hey, Grandmother," said Gluscabi, "I see. Now, how would one find that place where the wind eagle stands?"

Again Grandmother Woodchuck looked at Gluscabi. "Ah, Gluscabi," she said, "once again I feel that perhaps I should not tell you. But I know that you are very stubborn and would never stop asking. So I shall tell you. If you walk always facing the wind, you will come to the place where Wuchowsen stands."

"Thank you, Grandmother," said Gluscabi. He stepped out of the lodge, faced into the wind, and began to walk. He walked across the fields and through the woods, and the wind blew hard. He walked through the valleys and into the hills, and the wind blew harder still. He came to the foothills and began to climb, and the wind blew even harder.

Now the foothills were becoming mountains, and the wind was very strong. Soon there were no longer any trees, and the wind was very, very strong—so strong that it blew off Gluscabi's moccasins. But Gluscabi was very stubborn, and he kept on walking, leaning into the wind. Now the wind was so strong that it blew off his shirt, but he kept on walking. Now the wind was so strong that it blew off the rest of his clothes, and he was naked, but he still kept walking. Now the wind was so strong that it blew off his hair, but Gluscabi kept walking, facing into the wind.

The wind was so strong that it blew off his eyebrows, but still he continued to walk. Now the wind was so strong that he could hardly stand. He had to pull himself along by grabbing hold of the boulders. But there on the peak ahead of him he could see a great bird slowly flapping its wings. It was Wuchowsen, the wind eagle.

Gluscabi took a deep breath. "Grandfather!" he shouted.

The wind eagle stopped flapping his wings and looked around. "Who called me Grandfather?" he said.

Gluscabi stood up. "It's me, Grandfather. I just came up here to tell you that you do a very good job of making the wind blow."

The wind eagle puffed out his chest with pride. "You mean like this?" he said and flapped his wings even harder. The wind he made was so strong that it lifted Gluscabi right off his feet, and he would have been blown right off the mountain had he not reached out and grabbed a boulder.

"Grandfather!" Gluscabi shouted again.

The wind eagle stopped flapping his wings. "Yes?" he said.

Gluscabi stood up and came closer to Wuchowsen. "You do a very good job of making the wind blow, Grandfather. This is so. But it seems to me that you could do an even better job if you were on that peak over there."

The wind eagle looked toward the other peak. "That may be so," he said, "but how would I get from here to there?"

Gluscabi smiled. "Grandfather," he said, "I will carry you. Wait here." Then Gluscabi ran back down the mountain until he came to a big basswood tree. He stripped off its outer bark, and from the inner bark he braided a strong carrying strap, which he took back up the mountain to the wind eagle.

"Here, Grandfather," he said, "let me wrap this around you so I can lift you more easily." Then he wrapped the carrying strap so tightly around Wuchowsen that his wings were pulled flat against his sides and he could hardly breathe.

"Now, Grandfather," Gluscabi said, picking up the wind eagle, "I will take you to a better place." He began to walk toward the other peak, but as he walked, he came to a place where there was a large crevice. As he stepped over it, he let go of the carrying strap, and the wind eagle slid into the crevice, upside down, and was stuck.

"Now," Gluscabi said, "it is time to hunt some ducks." He walked back down the mountain, and there was no wind at all. He waited till he came to the tree line, and still no wind blew. He walked down to the foothills and down to the hills and the valleys, and still there was no wind. He walked through the forests and the fields, and the wind did not blow at all.

He walked and walked until he came back to the lodge by the water, and by now his hair and eyebrows had grown back. He put on some fine new clothing and a new pair of moccasins, took his bow and arrows, went down to the bay, and climbed into his boat to hunt ducks. Then Gluscabi paddled out into the water and sang his canoeing song:

Ki yo wah ji neh
Yo hey ho hey
Ki yo wah ji neh
Ki yo wah ji neh.

But the air was very hot and still, and he soon began to sweat. The air was so still and hot that it was hard to breathe. Soon the water began to grow dirty and smell bad, and there was so much foam on the water that he could hardly paddle. He was not pleased at all, and he returned to the shore and went straight to his grandmother's lodge. He walked in and said, "Grandmother, what is wrong? The air is hot and still, and it is making me sweat, and it is hard to breathe. The water is dirty and covered with foam. I cannot hunt ducks at all like this."

Grandmother Woodchuck looked up at Gluscabi. "Gluscabi," she said, "what have you done now?"

Gluscabi answered just as all children answer when asked that question. "Oh, nothing," he said.

"Gluscabi," said Grandmother Woodchuck again, "tell me what you have done."

Then Gluscabi told her about his visit to the wind eagle and what he had done to stop the wind.

"Oh, Gluscabi," said Grandmother Woodchuck, "will you never learn? Tabaldak, the Owner, set the wind eagle on that mountain to make the wind because we need the wind. The wind keeps the air cool and clean. The wind brings the clouds that give us rain to wash the earth. The wind moves the waters and keeps them fresh and sweet. Without the wind, life will not be good for us, for our children, or our children's children."

Gluscabi nodded his head. "*Kaamoji*, Grandmother," he said, "I understand."

Then he went outside. He faced in the direction from which the wind had once come and began to walk. He walked through the fields and the forests, and the wind did not blow, and he felt very hot. He walked through the valleys and up the hills, and there was no wind, and it was hard for him to breathe. He came to the foothills and began to climb, and he felt very hot and sweaty indeed.

At last he came to the mountain where the wind eagle had once stood, and he went and looked down into the crevice. There was Wuchowsen, the wind eagle, wedged upside down.

"Uncle?" Gluscabi called.

The wind eagle looked up as best he could. "Who calls me Uncle?"

he said.

"It is Gluscabi, Uncle. I'm up here. But what are you doing down there?"

"Oh, Gluscabi," said the wind eagle, "a very ugly naked boy with no hair told me that he would take me to the other peak so that I could do a better job of making the wind blow. He tied my wings and picked me up, but as he stepped over this crevice, he dropped me in, and I am stuck. And I am not comfortable here at all."

"Ah, Grandfather, er, Uncle, I will get you out," said Gluscabi. Then Gluscabi climbed down into the crevice. He pulled the wind eagle free and placed him back on his mountain and untied his wings.

"Uncle," Gluscabi said, "it is good that the wind should blow sometimes, and other times it is good that it should be still."

The wind eagle looked at Gluscabi and then nodded his head. "Grandson," he said, "I hear what you say."

So it is that sometimes there is wind, and sometimes it is still, to this very day. And so the story goes.

Joseph Bruchac of Greenfield Center, New York, is a storyteller and writer of Abenaki Indian and European ancestry. He is the co-author, with Michael Caduto, of Keepers of the Earth: Native American Stories and Environmental Activities for Children *(Fulcrum, 1988). Bruchac and his wife, Carol, live in the Adirondack foothills in the house where he was raised by his Abenaki grandfather.*

Jack and the Magic Boat

Ed Stivender

One morning Jack and his two brothers, Will and Tom, were sitting around the breakfast table. Jack said, "Pass me the milk, please." So they passed the milk to Jack. Jack looked at the milk carton, and on the side of the carton he saw a picture of a young girl with a crown on her head. Above the picture it said Missing Princess.

Below the picture it said, "Princess last seen being dragged into the woods under a spell by a wizard. One-thousand-dollar reward for her return."

Will said, "You know, Mama, I think I'll go out and dewitch that princess. Can you pack me a lunch?"

So Will's mama made him a lunch of roast chicken, chocolate cake, and a quart of milk, and she put it in a sack and sent him on his way. Will got halfway to the wizard's house, and he decided to sit down and have lunch. He was just about to start eating when all of a sudden an old woman with a staff in her hand came down the road and said, "Can you share some of your meal, sonny?"

Will looked up and said, "Oh no, old lady. I only have enough for myself. You're going to have to find your meal somewhere else." The old woman continued on her way.

Will finished what he could of his lunch—he wasted a lot of it, just threw it into the woods—and packed up and headed toward the wizard's house. When he got there, he knocked on the door, but there was no answer. All of a sudden he heard someone behind him say, "Yes, young man, what can I do for you this morning?"

Will turned around, and there was that evil-looking wizard, wearing his evil wizard clothes. Will said, "Well, sir, I'm here to dewitch the princess."

"If you want to dewitch the princess," the wizard said, "you're going to have to pass four tests. This is the first one."

The wizard brought out a hackle—a board about a foot square, with

Re-visioning this classic tale, I added the Smellwell character to three up the Hearwell/Seewell duo and balanced the battle a little by masculinizing the standard witch into a wizard and the helpful old man into a good witch. I think of this as a teaching tale about unity and diversity. As St. Paul says, "many gifts . . . one Spirit."

nails sticking up from it, that people use to beat flax to make linen. He placed the hackle on the ground, stood on a stump next to it, jumped into the air, came down headfirst on the hackle, and popped off without a scratch on him.

"Your turn," said the wizard.

Will stood on the stump, looked down, closed his eyes, jumped into the air, and came down headfirst on the hackle. Will screamed, "Oh, my head, my head, my head!" He ran home with blood streaming down his face. His mama fixed up his head with vinegar and brown paper, and Will was in bed for three weeks.

The next day it was brother Tom's turn. His mama packed him a lunch of roast chicken, chocolate cake, and a quart of milk, and she put it in a sack and sent him on his way. Tom got about halfway to the wizard's house, and he decided to sit down and have lunch. He was just about to start eating when all of a sudden an old woman with a staff in her hand came down the road and said, "Can you share some of your meal, sonny?"

Tom looked up and said, "Oh no, old woman. I only have enough for myself. You're going to have to find your meal somewhere else today." The old woman continued on her way.

Tom finished what he could of his lunch—he wasted a lot of it, just threw it into the woods—and packed up and headed toward the wizard's house. When he got there, he knocked on the door, but there was no answer. All of a sudden he heard someone behind him say, "Yes, young man, what can I do for you this morning?"

Tom turned around, saw the wizard, and said, "Well, sir, I'm here to dewitch the princess."

"If you want to dewitch the princess," the wizard said, "you're going to have to pass four tests. This is the first one."

He brought out the hackle, put it on the ground, stood on a stump next to it, jumped into the air, came down headfirst on the hackle, and popped off without a scratch on him.

"Your turn," said the wizard.

Tom stood on the stump, looked down, closed his eyes, and came down headfirst on the hackle. Tom screamed, "Oh, my head, my head, my head!" He ran home with blood streaming down his face. His mama fixed up his head with vinegar and brown paper, and Tom was in bed for three weeks.

The next day it was Jack's turn. Jack wasn't really the favorite of the family, and besides, his mama didn't have any more roast chicken and chocolate cake. So she packed him a lunch of two dried biscuits and a quart of tap water, and she put it in a sack and sent him on his way. Jack got about halfway to the wizard's house, and he decided to sit down and have lunch. He was just about to start eating when all of a sudden an old woman with a staff in her hand came down the road and said, "Can you share some of your meal, sonny?"

"Yes, ma'am, have a seat," said Jack. Then he gave the old woman one of his dried biscuits and half of his tap water.

When they were finished, the old woman said, "I can see you're an upstanding young man, Jack, and I've got a present for you." She reached into her pocket, pulled out a piece of tree bark, gave it to Jack, and said, "This is a piece of magic bark. All you've got to do is say, 'Sail, ship, sail,' and that piece of magic bark will take you wherever you want to go."

Jack thanked the old woman, said goodbye, and headed toward the wizard's house. But before he got there, he decided he'd try out his magic bark. He held it up and said, "Sail, ship, sail," and all of a sudden that bark began to expand and expand, until floating in the air in front of him was a 31-foot sailing ship with a mast reaching into the sky and sails flapping. The anchor was hooked onto a tree root.

Jack jumped into his magic boat, pulled in the anchor chain, and said, "Sail, ship, sail," and that ship went up and up and up. And soon Jack could see all over the countryside—his mama's house on one side, the wizard's house on the other. He decided he'd take a little ride around when all of a sudden he heard a sound.

He looked over the side of the boat, and down below there was a man running along the road as fast as he could—bumping his head into tree trunks so that all the leaves would shake off.

Jack yelled down to the man, "What's your name?"

"My name's Hardy Hardhead. What's yours?"

"My name's Jack. You want to come on my boat?"

"I'd love to."

So Hardy Hardhead got on the boat with Jack, and they sailed on. After a while Jack heard another sound. They looked over the side of the boat, and down below there was a man running through a meadow, stopping at ponds, and drinking them dry in one gulp.

Jack yelled down at the man, "What's your name?"

"My name's Drinkwell. What's yours?"

"My name's Jack. You want to come on my boat?"

"I'd love to."

So Drinkwell got on the boat with Jack and Hardy Hardhead, and they sailed on. After a while they heard another sound. They looked over the side of the boat, and down below there was a man running through a meadow, chasing sheep, catching them, and eating them whole.

Jack yelled down at the man, "What's your name?"

"My name's Eatwell. What's yours?"

"My name's Jack. You want to come on my boat?"

"I'd love to."

So Eatwell got on the boat. They were just about to sail away when all of a sudden they saw three young women standing on a grassy knoll.

The first young woman was listening, with her hand cupped over her ear. Jack said to her, "What do you hear?"

"I hear a monarch butterfly caterpillar chewing on a milkweed leaf a thousand miles away."

"What's your name?"

"Hearwell. What's yours?"

"My name's Jack. You want to come on my boat?"

"I'd love to."

So Hearwell got on the boat.

The second young woman was gazing into the distance, her hands shading her eyes. Jack said to her, "What do you see?"

"I see a raven swooping down to eat a monarch butterfly caterpillar chewing on a milkweed leaf a thousand miles away."

"What's your name?"

"Seewell. What's yours?"

"My name's Jack. You want to come on my boat?"

"I'd love to."

So Seewell got on the boat.

The third young woman was sniffing the air. Jack said to her, "What do you smell?"

"I smell raven's vomit. Those monarch butterfly caterpillars are poisonous, you know."

"What's your name?"

"Smellwell. What's yours?"

"My name's Jack. You want to come on my boat?"

"I'd love to."

So Smellwell got on the boat.

They were just about to sail away when—bang!—they heard a shot. They looked over the side of the boat, and there was a man with a rifle on his shoulder, and smoke was coming from its muzzle.

Jack said to him, "Hey, fella, what'd you just do?"

"I just put a raven out of his misery a thousand miles away."

"What's your name?"

"My name's Shootwell. What's yours?"

"My name's Jack. You want to come on my boat?"

"I'd love to."

So Shootwell got on the boat with Jack and the others, and they sailed on. After a while they heard another sound. They looked over the side of the boat, and down below was a young woman running so fast you could hardly see her. She was just a blur. Jack yelled down to her, "What's your name?"

"My name's Runwell. What's yours?"

"My name's Jack. You want to come on my boat?"

"I'd love to."

So Runwell got on the boat, and they sailed away. After a while Jack decided that it was time to visit the wizard. He took the boat down and down and down until it settled right there in the air in front of the wizard's house.

Jack got out of the boat, walked up to the front door, and knocked, but there was no answer. All of a sudden he heard someone behind him say, "Yes, young man, what can I do for you this afternoon?"

Jack turned around, saw the wizard, and said, "Well, sir, my friends and I have come to dewitch the princess."

"If you want to dewitch the princess," the wizard said, "You're going to have to pass four tests. This is the first one."

The wizard brought out the hackle, placed it on the ground, stood on the stump nearby, jumped into the air, came down headfirst on the hackle, and popped off without a scratch on him.

"Your turn," said the wizard.

"Well," said Jack, "I'd like my friend Hardy Hardhead to try that one."

Hardy Hardhead got out of the boat, stood on the stump, jumped into the air, flipped around twice, came down headfirst on the hackle, and broke it into a thousand pieces.

"So you've passed one of the four tests," the wizard said angrily. "There are still three more to go. And if you fail any of these three tests, I get to slit your throats from ear to ear and suck out your brains. Now, you got anybody who likes to drink?"

"Well," said Jack, "my friend Drinkwell loves to drink water."

Drinkwell got out of the boat.

"Drinkwell," said the wizard, "there are two creeks. That one will be yours, and this one is mine. We're going to race to see who can drink his creek dry first. If you win, you've passed two of the four tests. But if I win, I get to slit your throats from ear to ear and suck out your brains."

The wizard began to drink, but before he was half finished, Drinkwell had drunk his whole creek dry and had begun to drink from the headwaters of the wizard's.

"So you've passed two of the four tests," the wizard said. "There are still two more to go. You got anybody who likes to eat?"

"Well," said Jack, "my friend Eatwell loves to eat."

Eatwell got out of the boat.

The wizard disappeared behind his house and soon reappeared, holding two prize-winning cows by their horns. He handed one of the cows to Eatwell, saying, "We're going to race to see who can finish eating his cow first. If you win, you've passed three of the four tests, but if I win, I get to slit your throats from ear to ear and suck out your brains."

The wizard began to eat, but before he was half finished, Eatwell had finished his whole cow and said, "You got anything for dessert, sir?"

"All right, so you passed three of the four tests," the wizard said. "There's one more test to go. You got anybody who likes to run?"

"Well," said Jack, "my friend Runwell loves to run."

"We're going to race to see who can run the fastest from the Pacific Ocean and home again—3,000 miles over, 3,000 miles back."

The wizard broke an egg and let the yolk fall on the ground. He handed half of the eggshell to Runwell and said, "Fill your eggshell with saltwater to prove that you've been to the Pacific Ocean. If you win, we'll dewitch the princess. But if I win, I get to slit your throats from ear to ear and suck out your brains."

The wizard took off like a shot. Runwell passed him, ran all the way to the Pacific Ocean, filled her eggshell with saltwater, and headed home. She was about halfway back when she met the wizard running toward the Pacific Ocean.

The wizard knew he was going to have to pull a trick to win, so he reached in his pocket, pulled out a bottle of chloroform—that's a drug that makes you go to sleep—and poured some on a handkerchief. As Runwell was running by, he covered her mouth and nose with the handkerchief, and she fell down on the ground, asleep. The wizard left the handkerchief over her nose and ran on to the Pacific Ocean, knowing Runwell would never wake up.

Meanwhile, Jack and the gang became worried. Jack said to Smellwell, "What do you smell?"

"I smell chloroform, Jack, 1,500 miles away."

"Hearwell, what do you hear?"

"I hear snoring, Jack, 1,500 miles away."

"Seewell, what do you see?"

"Oh, Jack, it looks like Runwell is sleeping on the job. Her mouth and nose are covered with a handkerchief, and there's probably chloroform on it. She's never going to wake up."

"Not necessarily," said Shootwell, and he raised his rifle to his shoulder and pulled the trigger. Bang! The bullet traveled 1,500 miles and knocked the handkerchief away from Runwell's mouth and nose so she could breathe some fresh air. She woke up, looked around, saw her eggshell was empty, and headed back to the Pacific Ocean.

Meanwhile, the wizard was nearing the finish line when Runwell was seen on the horizon. She was running as fast as she could. Soon they were neck and neck, and finally Runwell, with her last ounce of energy, burst over the finish line and won the race.

The old wizard said, "You won fair and square, but oh, how I hate it when the good guys win." He led Jack and his friends behind his house to a shed and opened the door, and there was the princess, staring into space and saying, "B-A-T spells *cat*; C-A-T spells *bat* . . . "

"That's a spell, all right—a bad spell," said Jack.

The wizard waved his arms and said, "Abracadabra! The spell is lifted. Go back to your classroom for the gifted." The princess woke up.

Jack said, "Princess, we're here to take you home." So she got on the boat with Jack and his friends, and they sailed away until the boat settled in front of the castle. The king and queen ran out and hugged the princess, and together they all went into the castle.

The king gave Jack a thousand dollars. Jack and his friends spent the rest of the day just sailing in the magic boat and discussing how they could invest that thousand dollars so they could all live happily ever after.

Ed Stivender of Philadelphia is a member of Les Jongleurs de Notre Dame and marches in Philadelphia's Mummer's Day Parade. He has been the Henry Cadbury Speaker for the Friends' General Conference Gathering. Stivender is the author of Raised Catholic, Can You Tell? *(August House, 1992), a collection of coming-of-age stories.*

Knock, Knock, Who's There?

J. J. Reneaux

I wove this story from two family tales. In the first an ancestor washed up from her swampy grave and terrified her miserly husband. The second is about my great-aunt, whose mean papa refused her a doctor until it was too late. She died on the kitchen table as an unprepared country doctor attempted an emergency appendectomy.

Around La Ville—New Orleans, that is—the land is so low and wet that the dead have to be buried above the ground in vaults. Folks don't bury the dead in graves in the ground, oh no. If the river were to overflow the levee or a hurricane to flood the land, your loved one might just float back up from the grave and pay you a visit.

Down the river a little ways from La Ville there once lived an old man with his only child, a pretty girl named Thérèse. Her mama had died, leaving Thérèse in the care of her papa, a greedy, miserly man who worked his girl like a mule and dressed her in rags. Although she was of marrying age, he wouldn't allow any young man to court her. She saw no one except her mean old papa.

The only thing he cared for was the gold coins he kept hidden under a loose board in the floor beneath his bed. Every night he would lock his door, and by the light of a flickering candle he would count his golden coins. He loved the way they clinked and glowed and weighed so heavy in his hands.

But poor Thérèse was so lonesome. Every night she would come knocking on his door: *knock, knock.* Her papa would yell, "Who's there?"

"Papa, it's me, Thérèse. Papa, let me in; I'm so lonely. Talk to me."

But her papa would only holler back, "Girl, get out of here, and get back to work. You just want to get your hands on my gold, and that'll be over my dead body."

And so it went, until the night Thérèse fell ill. She rapped on the door as usual: *knock, knock.*

"Who's there?"

"Papa, it's me, Thérèse. I'm sick-sick," she said. "Papa, please let me in."

He yelled back, "You lazy good-for-nothing, get out of here. You're not sick; you just want to get your hands on my money, and that'll be over my dead body."

Again and again Thérèse returned to her papa's door and rapped:
knock, knock.

"Who's there?" he'd call.

"Papa, it's me. Please let me in—I'm bad sick. I need the healer,
Papa; please send for the *traiteur*."

Knock, knock.

"Who's there?"

"Papa, let me in; the pain is worse. Oh, Papa, open the door." But
her papa's heart was as cold as his golden coins. At last the girl's cries
faded to silence, and she knocked no more.

Then the old man was full of curiosity. But when he opened the
door, he found Thérèse lying lifeless on the porch floor.

Now, that old man was too stingy to buy a proper vault for his
daughter. Instead he laid Thérèse in a crude wooden coffin and buried
her in a shallow, swampy grave down by the cypress tree. The neighbors
shook their heads. They warned that there'd be trouble, for how could
poor Thérèse rest in peace in such a grave?

Three weeks went by, and a storm began to boil up over the gulf.
The winds churned, and the rain fell like needles as the hurricane
passed over the land. Night found that old man sitting in his room,
counting his gold coins by the flickering candlelight.

Outside the wind and rain pounded against the house. The old man
didn't know that the river had already spilled over the levee and sent its
dark water across the land. He sat in his rocking chair, his lap full of
gold, rocking and counting, "one, two, three . . . " Suddenly something
thumped up against his porch with a wooden clatter, and he heard a
sound at the door: *knock, knock.*

"Who's there?"

Only a great sigh like the wind answered.

Just a loose shutter, he thought, and he went on counting his shining gold, "one, two, three . . . "

More knocks on his door, stronger this time: *knock, knock.*

"Who's there?"

Only the whining wind answered him.

"It's just that good-for-nothing hound dog trying to get in." And he returned to counting his golden coins, "one, two, three . . . "

At that moment three great booming knocks hammered at his door: *knock, knock, knock!*

"Who's there?"

Only a sad, low moaning.

A shiver ran down the old man's back. "Storm's got me all jumpy. It's just the wind blowing that old live-oak tree, scraping its branches against the house."

But the moaning rose and rose above the howling wind until it became a horrifying scream: "Papa, it's me, Thérèse. Let me in. Papa, let me in. Let me in." And as the eye of the storm passed over the house, a blood-curdling shriek pierced the deadly calm.

Three days passed, and the waters receded. The neighbors came by to look in on the old man. As they rode onto his land and passed by the cypress tree, they saw that the flood had washed all the dirt away from Thérèse's grave, and it was empty.

They knocked at the back door, but nobody answered. Fearing that some harm had befallen the old man, they went inside. They found him sitting like stone in his rocking chair, cold as marble, his hair gone snow white, with a silent scream frozen on his lips and his glassy eyes bulged out in terror.

Across the room the door hung limp from one hinge as though some monstrous fist had pounded it down. Before it lay a battered, splintered coffin, and inside it was the gruesome corpse of Thérèse. Her withered hands clutched her papa's golden coins, and a ghastly smile was fixed on her decaying lips.

With the money the neighbors bought Thérèse a whitewashed vault and gave her a proper above-ground burial. But there wasn't enough money to buy the old man a vault, so they buried him in a pine coffin down by the cypress tree.

Since that time, whenever the river threatens to flood the land, the old man's troubled spirit rises to warn all that danger is at hand. Folks know he's paid them a visit when they hear *knock, knock, knock* at the door, and nobody is ever there.

J. J. Reneaux is a storyteller, writer, and musician. Best known for her Cajun folk tales, ghost lore, and family stories, Reneaux is the author of Cajun Folktales *(August House, 1992). She lives in Comer, Georgia.*

THE HERRING SHED

Jay O'Callahan

One summer my family and I vacationed in Pugwash, Nova Scotia. Our neighbor was an elderly farmer, Charlie Robertson, and through Charlie we met Maggie Thomas, who was 69 years old, blind, and infirm. I deeply admired both Maggie and Charlie's integrity, spirit, and laughter. This story was born of our friendship.

Nova Scotia. World War II. This is Cape Tormentine. That's the Northumberland Strait down there, and way beyond it is Prince Edward Island. It's six in the morning, spring here. All these people in the farmhouses around are up, and tonight they'll be turning on their radios to listen to the news about the war. We've all got people over there.

That's Maggie Thomas who just came out on the porch. She's 15. She worked in the herring shed last year, and the season's beginning again this morning—one hour from now, seven o'clock. She's the one to tell you about the herring shed.

I'm Maggie Thomas. I couldn't sleep last night. I was thinking about last season at the herring shed. I'll tell you, and you'll know why I couldn't sleep. I got to be down there in one hour. Oh, before I tell you, that's Papa's boat. See? Out in the strait with the brown-and-white sail. The best thing about the war is there's no gasoline, so you make your own sail. I helped Papa.

Well, let me tell you about last season. As a girl of 14, I was very, very keen to take on the work in the herring shed. In years before, my brother, Harry, had worked there, but he was fighting in the war so I got the job in the herring shed. At seven in the morning I stepped into the shed—Peg to my right, Mrs. Fraser across. Peg is 15, and she has long black braids and merry eyes, and Mrs. Fraser has the longest nose I ever saw and the nicest smile. She's my boss, a widow Mama's age.

"Maggie?"

"Yes, Mrs. Fraser."

"Now, Maggie, I know your brother, Harry, worked here, but just let me explain everything. The great big barrel outside—that's the pickle barrel, and the herring come right down on the slides. See? They're coming down now right onto the zinc table. You get on the rubber apron. That's it. You don't want to be wet because then you'll be cold. All right. Now, what you want to do is put 18 of the herring on the rod—it's called stringing it—and you put the rod on the rack there, and Corner Murdock will come and bring it to the drying shed. You know Corner?"

"Yes. He has a hole in his fence, so his cows are always on the corner."

"That's right. All day he's sipping at a vanilla bottle. Gets kind of silly. Pay no attention."

"I won't."

"Fine. Now, you pick up the rod like this, put your thumb in the gill, open it up, and slip the herring right onto the rod. Wait a minute. There's a rhythm: Thumb in the gill, open the mouth, slip it on the rod in the herring shed. Thumb in the gill, open the mouth, slip it on the rod in the herring shed. All right?"

"Yes. I can do it." I gave Peg and Mrs. Fraser a nod, and I picked up a rod and began the work in the herring shed. "Thumb in the gill, open the mouth, slip it on the floor . . . I'm sorry."

"Slow, Maggie. Slow. Slow."

"Yes, I will. Thumb in the gill, open the mouth. There, I got it on. Don't look at me. Thumb in the gill, open the mouth, slip it on. I've got it. I'm all right, Peg." Thumb in the gill, open the mouth, slip it on the rod in the herring shed. Thumb in the gill, open the mouth, I was doing the work in the herring shed. Eighteen on a rod, put the rod on the rack, pick up a rod without any slack, and go on with the work in the herring shed. Thumb in the gill, open the mouth, the hours passed by in the herring shed.

"Peg, I know we've got to do a lot for 45 cents, but how much?"

"What you do, Maggie, is a hundred rods. That's called a bundle, and that's about 45 cents."

"A hundred rods? That's 1,800 fish. It'll take me all summer."

"No, it won't. You'll do a bundle in a week or so. You're fast."

"I better get a lot faster." Thumb in the gill, open the mouth, slip it on the rod in the herring shed. Thumb in the gill, open the mouth, it was getting so cold in the herring shed. The floor was dirt, the sea to our backs, and the door was open so Corner Murdock could pick up the racks and bring them across to the drying shed.

"Peg, I don't want to complain my first day, but I can't feel my feet, my knees. Honest!"

"Well, it's almost lunch. Just dance or something. Go ahead."

"Well, I will." Thumb in the gill, open the mouth—I can't get it on the rod this way. Slip it on the rod in the herring shed. Thumb in the gill, open the mouth . . . oh, at last it was noon in the herring shed.

We stepped outside, and the sun was warm. Our lunch was a potato and a herring without its head. We talked of the war and the farms around and then went back to the cold, cold ground of the herring shed. Thumb in the gill, open the mouth, slip it on the rod in the herring shed. I finished the day, my very first day in the herring shed.

"Thank you, Peg. Thanks, Mrs. Fraser. A quarter. Oh, thank you. I'm faster than Harry."

I ran on home, straight by the sea, glad to be free of the cold of the herring shed. Charlie Robertson's wheat was tiny and green in the evening light, a sight to be seen.

"Hello, Charlie."

Charlie Robertson is the most wonderful farmer. He's the kindest man. You've got to say his name right—Charlie Robertson. He's a Scotsman and proud of it.

"Charlie, you didn't have to come over."

"Well, of course I did, Maggie. You finished the day. You did a bundle."

"Oh, I didn't do a bundle, Charlie, but I did more than half a bundle. I'm faster than Harry."

"Oh, of course you're faster than Harry. No question about that."

"I was looking at your wheat. It looks good."

"Well, you know, I told you. There are wet seasons and dry seasons and good seasons. It's going to be a good season."

"I think it will. I'm going to show my mother the quarter. I'll see you later."

"I hope so, Maggie."

I ran home, up the porch steps, but I didn't go in. I turned around, and I looked at the herring shed. It was my herring shed now. Not just Harry's and Mama's and everybody's. It was mine.

I was going to run in and say, "Look, Mama." It's silly, but we all do it. Mama's gone blind, the way her mama did and her mama before her. They say someday I might go blind. Anyway, I knew just where Mama would be. She'd be sitting on the couch, right by the fire, kneading the bread. I opened the door very quietly. I don't know what it was. Maybe it was making the quarter. Mama's pretty, and she's young, but she looks so frail.

"Mama! Open your hand."

"Maggie! You finished the day, dear. Come over. I'm so proud of you, Maggie. I know it's cold. And aren't they wonderful, Mrs. Fraser and Peg? I suppose Corner Murdock's still got his vanilla bottle. Don't tell your father. He doesn't think that's funny. All right? You can have my hand. A quarter! You're faster than Harry. You take it. You're wonderful. Oh, I hear your father, Maggie. You show it to him."

Well, Papa came in, and he was stringing the herring net across the room. It divided the room. He did it to mend the net. Papa doesn't frown, and he doesn't smile, but I knew he was proud of me.

"Look, Papa, a quarter. I'm faster than Harry; I'm faster. No, I want you to take it, Papa. I want you to take it. I'm helping like everybody."

Well, Papa took it, and that night for a change I did all the talking at supper. I told them about everything—about Mrs. Fraser and Peg and Corner Murdock and his vanilla bottle. Papa didn't think that was so funny. I was eating my chicken to the rhythm. Thumb in the gill, open the mouth, slip it on the rod in the herring shed. I must have sung it 50 times for Papa. Thumb in the gill, open the mouth, slip it on the rod in the herring shed.

"Thanks, Maggie, very much. I've got hold of it now."

"You're welcome, Papa."

After supper we did the dishes, and Papa went over and snapped the radio on. They were talking about Dunkirk, and so many people were killed there. Papa went over and snapped the radio right off because that's where we thought Harry was.

I've never gone to sleep so fast in my life. I dreamed of Harry, and he was far from dead. I could see him with that wild red hair, laughing at the cold in the herring shed.

At seven in the morning I was back in the shed—Peg to my right, Mrs. Fraser across. I gave them a nod, and I picked up a rod and went on with the work in the herring shed. Eighteen on a rod, put the rod on a rack, pick up a rod without any slack, and a week went by in the herring shed.

I was going fast one day, and Peg shouted, "You can do a bundle today, Maggie! Keep it up!"

"I will! I will!"

Thumb in the gill, open the mouth, slip it on the rod in the herring shed. Thumb in the gill, open the mouth . . . I did it! I did a bundle in the herring shed!

"Thank you, Mrs. Fraser. Forty-five cents. Thanks, Peg. See you later."

I was so happy and proud. And I'm glad it happened, because the next day was terrible in the herring shed.

We were working away. Thumb in the gill, open the mouth, and the rector came into the herring shed in his odd, shy way. The rector's got the worst job. He's 26 and has never been a rector before. Whenever anyone dies in the war, the station agent gives the telegram to the rector, and it's got so no one wants to see the rector coming up the path. Well, he's sandy-haired, and he leaned forward. "Maggie, could you come outside?"

I knew my brother, Harry, was dead. For a moment I couldn't move. I saw the telegram outside the shed. It was at Dunkirk.

"Thank you, Rector."

"I'm sorry, Maggie. I'm going to take you home."

"No . . . please. I don't want to go home. I'm sorry, Rector. I won't be any good to Mama like this. Let me get my feet on the ground. I would be very glad if you'd come tonight, Rector, with everybody."

And I went on with the work in the herring shed. Thumb in the gill, open the mouth, I went on with the work in the herring shed.

That night at home the neighbors came around. Mrs. Fraser brought pie; Peg brought bread. "Thanks, Mrs. Fraser. Come on, everybody. Sit down."

We must have had 30 people sitting in the kitchen. We just had the one kerosene lantern. People were telling funny stories and sad ones about Harry, and we were laughing and crying. All of a sudden the door opened, just about six inches.

"Mama! It's all right, Mama. It's Harry! It's Harry!"

I threw the door open and threw my arms around him. "Harry!"

"It's me, Corner Murdock, Maggie! It's Corner Murdock!"

"Oh, I'm sorry, Corner. I'm so sorry. Come on in."

Oh, I was so embarrassed. I wanted to run out into the night. Well, Mrs. Fraser took care of me, and Papa took care of Corner. Papa even gave Corner a whole bottle of vanilla. He never did that before.

I couldn't tell anyone why I did it. Well, I did it because of the way Corner opened the door. Ever since my brother, Harry, was about 8, he'd open the door six inches until everybody looked, and then he'd throw the door open and come in. That's what Corner had done.

I was so glad to be alone when everybody left. I went up to my room and looked out at the stars. "Why did you take him, God? Do you need him up there?"

And for hours I looked out into the blackness. I was looking at the strait, and I was trying to find the burning ship. For a hundred years, they say, there has been a burning ship out there. They say the people won't give up until they find a port.

Charlie Robertson saw it. Mama saw it before she went blind. And Harry saw it on his birthday. Well, it wasn't there.

At seven in the morning I was back in the shed—Peg to my right, Mrs. Fraser across. Peg held my hand, and Mrs. Fraser gave me a big hug. The strange thing was that I felt so numb, I just wanted to eat and sleep and work. So I went on with the work. Thumb in the gill, open the mouth, slip it on the rod in the herring shed. He lay in the ground, in the cold, cold ground, the ground that was cold as the herring shed. Thumb in the gill, open the mouth, slip it on the rod in the herring shed. Thumb in the gill, open the mouth, the weeks went by in the herring shed. Thumb in the gill, open the mouth . . . I didn't realize it, but I was so fast one day, Peg shouted, "You can do two bundles, Maggie!"

"I will! I will!"

Thumb in the gill, open the mouth, slip it on the rod in the herring shed. Eighteen on a rod, a hundred to a bundle, 45 cents. I did it. I did two bundles in the herring shed.

"Oh, thank you so much. Ninety cents, Mrs. Fraser. We'll buy a whole herd of cows. I'll see you later."

I ran on home, straight by the sea, glad to be free of the cold of the herring shed. Charlie Robertson's wheat was tall and green in the evening light, a sight to be seen.

"Hello, Charlie."

"Hello, Maggie. You were looking pretty far down there for a while. Good to see you."

"Oh, we're better. We're much better. Honest. We still wake up crying, and Mama says we'll do that for a year. Oh, Charlie, thank you for everything you and Margaret sent—all the meat and vegetables."

"Oh, listen, would've gone to rot at my place."

"They wouldn't have gone to rot, Charlie. You're wonderful. We talk about you all the time. Charlie, can I ask you something?"

"Well, I hope so, Maggie. What is it?"

"Were you ever lonely when you were my age?"

"Oh, I was lonely all right. I don't remember so much about being 14 and 15, but I was lonely. When I was 9, 10, 11, I had nobody to play with. I used to go outside. Who was I going to play with? Jimmy Davis's boy? Little brat. I wouldn't play with him. I made up an imaginary friend. Nobody could see him but me. Jimmy Scotsman. He was enormous, had big shoulders. I'd come out, and I'd say, 'Jimmy Scotsman, take my hand.' As soon as he took my hand, I was 19, enormous."

"I want to meet someone like that but someone real."

"Oh, you will, Maggie."

"I don't think so. Papa doesn't approve of dances. He says I can never go to a dance."

"There are other ways of meeting someone."

"Do you think I'm pretty?"

"I think you're pretty, Maggie. I think you're pretty wonderful."

"Thank you. I'll see you later."

"Well, I hope so, Maggie."

Thumb in the gill, open the mouth, slip it on the rod in the herring shed. The weeks passed by in the herring shed. Thumb in the gill, open the mouth, slip it on the rod in the herring shed.

One day I must have had a good sleep or something because I was flyin'. By ten-thirty I had done a bundle, and Peg shouted at me, "Maggie, you can do three bundles today! You might never do it again, but you can do three today!"

"I will! I will!"

Thumb in the gill, open the mouth, slip it on the rod in the herring shed.

"Peg, I'm not going to have lunch. Get a potato, and stick it in my mouth."

Thumb in the gill, open the mouth, slip it on the rod in the herring shed. By two o'clock I could barely move, but I was going to do three bundles that day. I kept at it. Thumb in the gill, open the mouth, slip it on the rod in the herring shed. Thumb in the gill, open the mouth . . . I did it! I did three bundles in the herring shed.

"Oh, I'm so proud, Mrs. Fraser. I never thought I'd do it. A dollar thirty-five. We can buy a new farmhouse. Oh, thank you. I'll see you later."

Well, it was a wonderful day. I felt so good. But the next morning when I got there, I was so stiff I could barely pick the rod up. I picked it up, and I felt awful giddy, so I started laughing and pretending I couldn't even get the fish on. I pretended to groan. Thumb in the gill, open the mouth . . . Well, Peg started laughing, and the two of us were laughing, pretending we couldn't get the fish on. Thumb in the gill, open the mouth . . . We looked at Mrs. Fraser, and we were trying to make her laugh, but nothing breaks her concentration. Her hands are like fairies gone mad. Thumb in the gill, open the mouth, slip it on the rod in the herring shed. Thumb in the gill, open the mouth, slip it on the rod in the herring shed.

The two of us bent over, calling, "Mrs. Fraser." We said it slow as molasses. Thumb in the gill, open the mouth . . . We saw the littlest bit of a smile, and we knew we had her. Peg picked up her black braids and pretended she was an opera star. Thumb in the gill, open the mouth . . . And I bent over with my rod. "Mrs. Fraser." Thumb in the gill, open the mouth . . . She couldn't resist us. She dropped the rod, and she bent back and started laughing and clapping. And we danced around. Thumb in the gill, open the mouth, slip it on the rod in the herring shed.

We were dancing around, and Corner Murdock came in. He looked like an elephant's trunk, and he bent over and picked up the drying rack, and all of a sudden Peg got one arm, and I got the other. Thumb in the gill, open the mouth, and we danced around with him. I was dancing with a man, even if it was Corner. Thumb in the gill, open the mouth, slip it on the rod in the herring shed.

"All right now," Corner said wildly. "Thank you very much. That's enough."

We wouldn't let him go, and he stared at Mrs. Fraser. She picked up a rod and pretended she was conducting. Thumb in the gill, open the mouth . . . Well, poor Corner Murdock dropped the rack and ran outside, and with all of us watching, he opened his vanilla bottle and drank it down. Oh, we laughed and danced and sang, and Mrs. Fraser told stories about her grandmother. And we worked too. I made 6 cents that day. It was the most wonderful day of the whole summer, and it was good that it was, because the next two days were the worst.

We were back to normal the next day. We were working away at 10 o'clock. Thumb in the gill, open the mouth, and the rector came into the herring shed. He leaned forward in that shy way. "Mrs. Fraser, will you come outside?" She came right around the zinc table. She wasn't going out.

"It's one of my sons, isn't it? Dead?"

"I'm sorry. It's Jack."

"Oh, God!"

She wept right in front of us, and then she straightened up, and she cried, "Well, please God, if it has to be one, it should be Jack! Gannett's got a wife and a son. You know that."

"I've got the car outside. I'll take you home."

"I'm not going home, Rector. Thank you. There's no one at home. I'll finish the way Maggie did. But I'll be very glad if you come tonight with everybody."

And she went on with the work in the herring shed. Thumb in the gill, open the mouth, the war came home to the herring shed.

I ran on home, straight by the sea, glad to be free of the cold of the herring shed.

"Hello, Charlie."

"I'm sorry, Maggie. Sad day. Is she all right?"

"She's a strong woman, Charlie. She kept working to the end. We'll see you there tonight. We'll bring the chicken."

"We'll bring the scalloped potatoes."

"See you later, Charlie."

"Well, I hope so, Maggie."

At seven in the morning we were back in the shed—Peg to my right, Mrs. Fraser across. She came to work despite her loss, and we went on with the work in the herring shed. Thumb in the gill, open the mouth . . . The rector came in at 10 o'clock, and Mrs. Fraser came right around.

"Rector, very kind of you, but I'll be all right now. I've got Peg and Maggie here, and at least Gannett's alive."

And the rector was still.

"Gannett's alive, isn't he?" she cried out. "Gannett's alive?"

"No, he's dead."

"God! Oh, God!"

And she fell to the floor in the herring shed. She was taken on home and put to bed, and we went on with the work. Thumb in the gill, open the mouth, slip it on the rod in the herring shed. We went on with the work in the herring shed. I ran on home, straight by the sea, glad to be free of the cold of the herring shed, and I swore I would never go back there. It was too cold, and it was too sad. I'd make money some other way.

"Hello, Charlie. Don't want to talk, Charlie. I'll see you there tonight."

We paid Mrs. Fraser another evening call and brought food. Then we went home, and Papa turned on the radio. Mr. Churchill was speaking, and he sounded so strong. His words were old and simple and bold: "We shall not flag or fail. We shall go on to the end . . . . we shall fight on the beaches, we shall fight on the landing grounds, we shall fight in the fields and in the streets, we shall fight in the hills. We shall never surrender." We sat at the table, and our eyes were wet, and I looked at Papa, and his fists were set. Papa stood up, and then he smashed the table with his fist and cried, "Damn it, Maggie! We'll go on to the end!"

At seven in the morning I was back in the shed—Peg to my right, and Mrs. Fraser came in. She looked so old and so thin. But she gave us a nod and went on with the work. Thumb in the gill, open the mouth, slip it on the rod in the herring shed. The herring that are dried are put on the ships and sent to England for hungry lips. We went on with the work in the herring shed. Oh, we went on, yes, we went on; dear God, we went on with the work in the herring shed.

Well, the season finally ended, and I was so glad. I stood outside until Corner Murdock snapped the lock, and it was done.

It was harvest season. Everyone had to help, even Mrs. Fraser. You couldn't be too sad. And finally winter came, and I'll never forget. It snowed all day and all night, and Mama said we'd find the laughter underneath the snow. She was right. Sometimes there would be six or seven people sitting around the kitchen at night, telling stories. It was fun outside too. I built a snowman one day.

"Charlie! Charlie! Who do you think the snowman is?"

"I don't know, Maggie."

"It's you."

"Well, I thought so."

"You did not."

"Well, listen. Your father doing the cutting?"

"He's cutting, all right. Four cords of wood for you on Friday."

"What about the grain?"

"He's going to bring the grain over as soon as the ice is hard. Let's have a snowball fight."

"I think I'll pass it up, Maggie."

"I'll see you later."

"Well, I hope so, Maggie."

I wanted the winter to go on forever. But it's over. You can smell the air this morning. It's spring. Oh—it must be seven o'clock. I'm going to have to hurry! That's Peg going into the herring shed. Mrs. Fraser's already there. Well, now you know why I couldn't sleep. But before I go, that's Papa's boat you see down there. I told you the best thing about the war is there's no gasoline. You make your own sails. I helped Papa make those. Well, I've got to go. I'll see you later.

Thumb in the gill, open the mouth, slip it on the rod in the herring shed. Eighteen in a row, a hundred in a bundle, 45 cents. We'll go on with the work in the herring shed.

"Hello, Mrs. Fraser. Nice to see you. Hello, Peg. Your braids look so nice. Mrs. Fraser, you'll have to tell stories again this year. Oh, I'll never be as fast as you."

The herring that are dried are put on the ships and sent to England for hungry lips. We'll go on with the work in the herring shed. Thumb in the gill, open the mouth, slip it on the rod in the herring shed. Thumb in the gill, open the mouth, that is my tale of the herring shed.

Jay O'Callahan of Marshfield, Massachusetts, has performed from Lincoln Center to Stonehenge, from the Cultural Center in Niger to Dublin's Abbey Theatre. He has been commissioned to write stories for cities, towns, and orchestras. O'Callahan's sound recordings and videotapes have won numerous awards from such organizations as the Parents' Choice Foundation, the American Library Association, and the Birmingham International Educational Film Festival.

The Selma Tourists

Kathryn Windham

My daddy always said the truth is hard to beat. This story is absolutely true, and I tell it just the way it happened.

Selma, Alabama, is a nice little town. The funniest things sometimes happen in Selma, though.

In 1967, not long after the 1965 marches and civil-rights demonstrations, we decided that the town needed a more positive image. We figured that we should let the whole country know that Selma was indeed a pleasant town to visit.

The chamber of commerce got together and decided that they'd put on a special promotion to try to lure some tourists into Selma and then show them the time of their lives. The members of the chamber decided they were going to stop a carload of "typical tourists" on the edge of town and give them a weekend of Selma-style Southern hospitality at its finest.

Well, on the appointed day the police car was all waxed and shining. Red Pyron, a tall red-headed man and the police captain at the time, was out by the road, looking both official and pleasant. The reigning Miss Central Alabama was there, and so were the mayor and the president of the chamber of commerce, and several more who made up the welcoming committee. Everyone was gathered just off Highway 80 East across the river bridge at a traffic light. As people drove into town and stopped at the light, we could kind of look them over and then select a fine-looking family to be the city's guests.

Well, we let a lot of cars go by for one reason or another—the children were rowdy or the cars were dirty and dented, things like that. After a while, though, here came a new-model automobile with the perfect tourists inside: a nice-looking man and woman in the front seat and a lovely little girl in the back. "They're it," we all agreed.

Red blew the siren on the police car. The man pulled over and looked a little startled, but Red said, "Oh, you haven't done anything wrong. We just want your family to be the guests of Selma for the weekend." He explained about our typical-tourists promotion and asked if they would honor Selma by accepting that title and its attendant benefits.

The man said, "Well, let me see what my wife thinks about that." They conferred a little bit, and then they said, "Well, we were on our way to Texas for a vacation, but this sounds like it might be nice."

We escorted them to the Holiday Inn, which already had up on its marquee WELCOME TYPICAL TOURISTS. Talk about coverage—we had most of the local television stations, all the state news outlets, and the Associated Press and United Press International there. We never had been as grand to visitors as we were to these three.

They were delightful people. The man said he had a chain of filling stations in North Carolina, and he showed us some photographs of them. One snapshot showed his wife pumping gas. He said it was just a gag shot, though. His wife really stayed at home and took care of their little girl. That was important, he said—bringing up a child right. The little girl had the nicest manners too—said, "yes, ma'am," "no, ma'am," "please," and "thank you."

Our typical tourists said, "Oh, this is such a friendly town." The fellow even said he might want to open a branch filling station in Selma, which is the kind of talk chambers of commerce love.

Well, we had barbecues for them, and we took them boating on the river, and we took them to all the historic homes, and we left no stone unturned for the finest weekend we could provide.

Well, Monday morning came, and we said to ourselves, "Good. They can go on to Texas; we've been our pleasant selves now, and we can get back to normal." We went to tell our typical tourists goodbye, and the man said, "Everybody's been so nice to us here in Selma. We'd like to go thank all the merchants for the nice things they've given us." We thought, *Now, isn't that just the nicest thing you've ever heard.*

So they went downtown and started off with the Jackson Clothing

Store. Mr. Jackson had sent the man a shirt and tie. There was a nice sport coat in the window, and the man said to his wife, "That's just the kind of sport coat I've been looking for. It'd be just right for me to wear in Texas." He said, "I wish I could buy it, but we've spent most of our cash, so I guess I won't be able to."

Mr. Jackson overheard him and said, "That's all right—we'll be glad to take your check."

The man said, "Would you mind if I made the check for just a little bit more than the cost of the coat? I'm a little short of cash."

Mr. Jackson said, "That would be just fine." So he took his check, and the man took his sport coat.

Well, they went on down to Bewig's Jewelry. Mr. Bewig had sent the woman a pretty bracelet, so she thanked him, and right there in the showcase was a watch like she said she had always wanted. She said, "Honey, I wish I could have that watch." He said, "Well, you know we really can't buy it now because I don't have that much cash, and we've got to go to Texas." Mr. Bewig said, "Oh, we'll be glad to take your check."

The man said, "Well, would it be all right if I just wrote it for a little bit more than the cost of the watch?"

"That's fine," said Mr. Bewig. So the man wrote his check, and they took the watch.

They went all over town doing this, thanking people for scarves and shoes and whatnot. That man and woman were so gracious about thanking everybody, and everywhere they went, they got a little check cashed and bought a little merchandise.

Well, by then it was lunchtime, and we had to feed them again, but that was okay. We figured it was worth it for the good feeling we were building about Selma.

Finally they left town, and as soon as they did, we all collapsed. We had been pleasant as long as anybody could be expected to be. But we were mighty proud because the plan had been just as successful as could be. We'd gotten loads of publicity, and it was all good. We spent the next few days congratulating one another on what a fine promotion it had been.

About the time we were feeling rested up, some unsettling news arrived from North Carolina. Those checks the typical tourists had written in Selma started coming back, stamped "No account." Bank officials in North Carolina said that our visitors had written a cascade of worthless checks in eight or 10, maybe 12 states.

That wasn't the worst of it. It turns out that the three of them were traveling in a stolen car. The man was an escaped convict. The woman was not his wife. We don't know where the child fit in.

So if you come to Selma, we'll be very glad to see you. But don't try to get any checks cashed.

Kathryn Windham was the first dues-paying member of the National Association for the Preservation and Perpetuation of Storytelling and served on its board of directors for eight years. She has three children and two grandsons and lives in Selma, Alabama, where she collects insulators, dirt-dauber nests, doorknobs, and stories.

JACK AND THE THREE STEERS

Ray Hicks

Jack and his mother was without flour and had nothing to eat. So he said, "Mama," he said, "I believe I can make it and get us something to eat." So he headed off. She let him go. Looked like he'd have to go to put food on the table.

He headed off and got lost in the woods—dark woods—dark even in the daytime. It come night on him, and it let in raining. He kept crawling around in the woods, and finally he looked, and he saw a little light down in a holler, a-shining way down in a lonesome holler through the dark. So he kept pulling and got there.

When he got there, he pecked on the door, and a little woman come out. She said, "Law me! What is you a-doing here?" She said, "This is the highway robbers' house. And, son, they kill everybody that comes here. They say dead men tells no tales."

Well, he stood there and talked with her awhile in the rain, and he was a-getting so wet, and he said, "Well, bedad, I'm a-coming in! I'd just as soon be killed as to drown out here." She said, "Well, come on in then, just as you please." There was a little pile of straw a-laying over in the room. Jack was wet and drowsy, so he went over and laid down in that little pile of straw, and he got warm and went off to sleep.

At midnight the robbers came in with their stuff and put their guns out on the table and was a-dividing what money they'd got and other stuff. Jack rousted and made a mumble of a fuss. They said, "What's that, old lady?"

"Oh," she said, "I forgot to tell you-uns. It was a little old boy come in. I told him that you-uns would kill him, but he said he'd just as soon be killed as to drown out there in the rain."

The robbers said, "Get up. What's your name?" Jack said, "My name's Jack." They said, "Well, we kill everybody that comes here. Dead people tells no tales."

Well, Jack was ragged and looked pitiful, and he said, "Well, I ain't got nothing." He said, "You-uns is robbers, no doubt, and a-robbing for what you get, but if you rob me and kill me, you don't get nothing. Me and my mother is without anything to eat, is why I'm out like this."

Well, they got to looking at him and got sort of sorry for him. They said, "Jack, do you reckon you would be a good hand to steal?" Jack said, "Bedad, a man ought to be a good hand if it would save his life."

"Well," they said, "it could save it. There's an old farmer back over yonder. He's got three steers, and we've tried every way to steal them, but we can't get them." They said, "We was a-figuring on trying tomorrow, but being as you've happened to be here, if you'll get them for us, we'll give you $300 apiece and spare your life. In the morning he'll be a-taking the first one to town."

Well, Jack got to feeling awful bad about it, thinking that he was a-going to be killed—that he would fail. But the next morning he went down by the lower end of the house, and the robbers had had a calf or something tied up there and had forgot and left the rope. So Jack snatched the rope off of the pin and wrapped it around him and went on down to the road where the farmer was a-driving the ox to town to sell it. Jack looked up and saw a stooping tree and said, "Ah, bedad," he said, "I might fool that old man and not have to hurt nobody to get that steer."

He climbed that stooping tree over the road and rolled the rope around him and fixed it and got it around his neck like he was hung. He hung there, and the old farmer come along, saying, "Sook, Buck; saw, Buck, let's get to town." He got on around that turn where Jack was a-hanging, and he looked—said, "Law me! I'll not get to town today. It'll be a funeral!" And said, "No doubt that them robbers has hung this boy. I better just tie my ox and get my neighbors and get him down, and it'll be a funeral in place of going to town." Said, "I'll just tie this ox here now, and I'll get him directly."

Well, he tied his ox and struck back and told it all over the community that the robbers had hung a boy in a tree, and he had about 50 or a hundred men a-going with him.

Just as quick as the farmer got out of sight, Jack untied and got the steer and struck up to the robbers' and was back with it in about two or three hours. The robbers said, "Good gracious." They said, "You're the best hand to steal that's ever been on this job. You're a-doing well."

Jack said, "Bedad, a man has to do something if it will save his life." And he said, "I don't believe in hurting nobody."

"Well," they said, "you'll go for the next one in the morning." Jack never slept too much that night. He worried, a-studying yet, because it was still two to go, and he didn't know how he would get them.

He got up the next morning, and there laid a brand-new woman's slipper where they'd dropped it on the floor. Jack snatched it and put it in his pocket. Then he got down to the road. Directly he heard the old farmer a-coming with the second steer. "Sook, Buck; saw, Buck, let's get to town before the market closes." When he heard him a-coming pretty close, he eased out and throwed that slipper into the road.

The old farmer come up and said, "Saw, Buck! Saw, Buck!" He looked and picked it up, said, "Law me!" Said, "There's a brand-new slipper them robbers has lost. If I had the mate to that, I believe they'd be exactly to fit for my old lady." Said, "Just her fit, no doubt, but it wouldn't be any use without the mate to it."

Well, he threw the slipper back down, said, "Sook, Buck, let's get to town," and started on. He forgot to notice which foot it went on—never paid any attention. Jack went out and grabbed it and took a near-cut through the woods, about a mile ahead, and set the slipper down in the road again.

The farmer said, "Sook, Buck; saw, Buck!" Said, "Law me! Ain't I a fool. There is the mate to that shoe, and me a mile on this-a-way. I ought to have put the other one in my pocket." Said, "They've lost one back there, and they've lost the other one here."

So he said, "Saw, Buck," and tied him up and grabbed that slipper up and run back to get the other one. He got mistaken in which place the other one was laying and got excited, and he run around with his tongue a-hanging out, saying, "It looked like it was right here, where I saw that slipper. No, it was up there." And he'd run there. "No, I believe it was that turn right back down yonder." Then when he went back, his steer was gone. By that time Jack had that steer and was back at the robbers'.

They said, "Great, Jack! You're the best!" Said, "You've done made $600 already, and you're a-savin' your life! Now, in the morning is the third one." Said, "You bring it, and we'll give you 900 bucks, and your life is saved. We won't hurt you, just to keep your mouth shut about us."

Well, Jack went back and just sat down, and he couldn't figure on anything to get that last one with. Finally he heard the farmer a-coming. "Sook, Buck; saw, Buck, get to town." Jack had to think of something, or he was gone.

Then he happened to think that he could get up in the laurel and bawl like two steers and get the farmer up in there after him and dodge him like a rabbit. So he went up in the laurel, said, "Moo, maw! Moo, maw!"

The farmer said, "Just as I expected, they got loose. I'll get up in there and catch the other two and take them all three on to market today."

So he got up in there after Jack, and he jumped across that laurel and kept after him. Heard "Moo!" on one ridge—"Yeah, that's them," he said. Then Jack—he'd rabbit-hunted a lot—would give him a dodge like a rabbit, and he got him tangled with his britches under some thick laurel and spikes in his britches and him there a-pulling and hung up. Jack jumped out and got the steer and took it while the farmer was a-getting out of them greenbriars and that laurel.

Well, the robbers paid Jack the $900. He went back home, and him and his mother lived good for a while.

Ray Hicks, the patriarch of traditional storytelling in America, was named a National Heritage Fellow by the National Endowment for the Arts in 1983. Hicks, a farmer, lives in Banner Elk, North Carolina.

THE TALE OF DAME RAGNEL

Heather Forest

King *Arthur hunted in a deep dark wood,*
And there he saw the strangest sight.
A castle loomed before him,
And its towers were black as night.

Suddenly King Arthur heard a rustling sound behind him, and he turned to see a great deer leap across his path. Just as he was about to claim his prey, a knight, dressed entirely in black armor, came riding from the eerie castle in full battle array. The knight drew his silvery sword and said, "You hunt on my lands. I shall have your head."

"Wait!" cried Arthur. "I am not dressed for battle, and I have no sword at my side. If you strike me down unarmed and my royal life you claim, from every court in this kingdom you will be banished with shame. Let me leave. I give you my word that I will return with my sword, Excalibur, at my side. Then our fight will be fair. Allow me to go and return, if you dare."

"Very well," said the knight, lowering his sword. "I will not strike now. You may leave, but return to this place one year from today without a sword, dressed as you are now. Come armed only with the answer to a riddle I shall give. If you can bring me an answer that is acceptable to most, I will let you live."

"I give you my word that I will return as you say. Now give me your riddle. I can solve any," Arthur said boastfully.

"You won't easily solve this one," said the knight with a grin. "What is it that women want most?"

Arthur laughed. "That is easy to solve. I will ask every female in the kingdom if I must. I will return with an answer one year from today."

But when Arthur asked every girl child, every maiden, every mother, every grandmother, every beldame in the kingdom what it was

This story was

an old Breton lay,

a minstrel's song,

centuries before

Chaucer included

his version,

"The Wife of Bath,"

in The Canterbury

Tales *and*

John Gower wrote it

into his Tale of

Florent *in the 1300s.*

These and a

15th-century monk's

manuscript provided

the threads from

which I wove

my version of

the tale.

167

that women want most, everyone gave him a different answer.

One woman said, "Beauty."

Another told him, "Youth."

"Children," someone else offered.

"Grandchildren," came yet another reply.

"No, no!" argued someone else still. "What women want most is sleep."

No one agreed. So Arthur found himself riding toward the strange castle one year from that dreadful day without a single answer that would be acceptable to most. As he rode, without a sword and dressed in his hunting greens, toward what he supposed would be his own cruel death, he heard fairies singing. There in an opening in the glen, he saw fairy women dancing around a mound.

And we'll sing all day
For the sun in the sky
Till the sun goes down
And the moon rises up
With stars for a crown.
Then we'll dance all night
For the stars and the moon
Till the sun shines on,
And we'll sing for the dawn.

The creatures were so beautiful, he turned away in disbelief. When he looked up again, they were gone. But in the center of the circle where they had been dancing, he saw the most wretched hag of a woman he had ever beheld.

Her hands were bent and gnarled. Her skin was so wrinkled that it looked like the bottom of a dry riverbed, long since gone barren. Her hair stuck up like wiry spikes. She had few teeth. She was covered with open sores. She was dressed in animal skins, and she smelled horrible.

"Greetings, Arthur. My name is Dame Ragnel. And I have the answer to the riddle you seek. Allow me, great king, to speak."

"If you have the answer to the riddle, please tell me. I ride unarmed to my death."

"Not so quickly," she said. "If I give you the answer that saves you, Sire, will you give me my heart's desire?"

"I will give you anything you want."

She leaned close to him and whispered the answer in his ear.

"Of course!" he said when he heard her words. "As a man, I would want no less for myself." Much braver of heart, he mounted his horse and set out for the castle.

The knight rode out to greet him, once again dressed all in black. His sword drawn high above his head, he cried, "I will strike now!"

"Wait! I have an answer," Arthur replied. He breathed deeply and recalled the words the hag had given him. "What women want most is their own sovereignty—the right to rule themselves, to do with their lives as they wish."

"How could you have known that?" shrieked the knight. "My stepsister, Dame Ragnel, must have told you!"

The knight broke apart into 10,000 shards of stone, and the castle cracked and vanished. Arthur stood alone in the swirling mists and saw the hag walking toward him.

She said, "I see that you are alive. All I want in return is the finest knight in all the realm to be my husband."

Although Arthur was perplexed at her request, he thought, *Surely my knights would give their lives in battle. Why not in marriage?*

He lifted the hag onto his horse, and together they rode back to his castle. The knights of the Round Table, Queen Guinevere, and all the fair ladies of the court gathered round to hear Arthur's tale of how Dame Ragnel had saved his life with the answer to a riddle. Everyone gasped when he said, "In return she wants the finest knight in all the realm to be her husband."

No one stirred as Dame Ragnel walked slowly past the knights. She passed Sir Lancelot and Sir Kay, and she stopped at Sir Gawain. "I want you," she said.

"Oh! It isn't fair," said one of the fine ladies of the court. "Sir Gawain is the youngest, the handsomest, the noblest, the bravest in battle. Why, I myself had my heart set upon him."

But Gawain's allegiance was first to his king. He knelt before the hag and said, "You have saved my king's life. Will you be my wife?"

She agreed, and the wedding took place that very day. It was not a festive affair. No one had much appetite except Dame Ragnel, who ripped meat from the roasts with her hands and ate rudely, the grease dripping from her chin.

After the celebration Dame Ragnel and Sir Gawain retired to his chambers. She stood before him, still dressed in her animal skins, for she would not trade them for a wedding gown, and said, "Gawain, sweet husband, I am your wife. Kiss me."

He hesitated for a moment. She said, "So, you refuse your bride on her wedding night? You are not as chivalrous as they say."

Now, to call a knight of the Round Table unchivalrous was a far greater insult than to call him a coward in battle. For in those days, to hold a woman in the highest esteem was considered a great virtue.

Gawain tried to excuse his poor behavior, saying, "Please forgive me. I hesitated, but I had my reasons. You're not rich, you're not of noble birth, and you're not young."

"Gawain," she said, "look into my eyes. See who I really am." And then she said:

Nobility is not borne in the blood of the child,
Passed down to daughter or son.
True nobility comes from the deeds of one's life,
From the good that has been done.
And of wealth? Look at this castle! A prison,
Bolted and barred with fright.
I prefer my poor hovel in the woods,
Where I have no fear of thieves in the night.
And as for youth? It's true I have turned that page.
But I offer you the beauty and wisdom of my age.

Gawain was moved by her words. He reached for Dame Ragnel's gnarled hand, gently lifted it to his lips, and kissed her. When he drew back, he saw that no hag stood before him at all! In her place stood the most beautiful maiden in the blush of youth that he had ever seen.

"What kind of sorcery is this?" he cried. "I want nothing to do with the black arts."

"Gawain, do not refuse me now that I am finally in my rightful form! It was no sorcery of mine that you've beheld this day but that of my evil stepmother. She bewitched my stepbrother to challenge visitors and give them strange riddles to solve. She enchanted me to be a hag until the finest knight in all the realm agreed to be my husband of his own free will. With that kiss, Gawain, you broke half the spell."

"Half?" he asked.

"Yes. Now you have a choice. Think carefully. You may have me as a beauty by day for all the world to see and a hag by night in the privacy of our chambers. Or you may have me be a hag by day and a beauty by night. How would you have me?"

"This is a difficult choice," said Gawain. "But since it has everything to do with your own happiness, it is no choice for me to make at all. I have looked into your eyes, and I've seen the true beauty within you. I will have you however you choose to be."

"So," she said with a laugh, "I have my sovereignty—the right to rule myself, to do with my life as I wish! You have broken the spell entirely. And now I choose to remain in my rightful youthful form till time comes and turns my hair white."

Well, a thousand kisses were none too many to celebrate their wedding that night.

Heather Forest is a storyteller, singer, and writer who has produced five albums of tales and two children's books. Her stories appear in four storytelling anthologies and are aired frequently on children's radio programs. Forest has performed at festivals and in theaters for audiences of all ages since 1974. She lives in Huntington, New York.

THE WHOLE LOAD

Waddie Mitchell

In a Western town in the days of old,
'Fore the mines closed down for the lack of gold,
The folks there seized opportunity
And built them a right smart community.
They built them a school, where the R's were taught,
And they built them a church on a corner lot.
They painted her white, with a steeple high
To greet town folk as they's passin' by.

They had 'em a sheriff, a judge, and a mayor,
But they needed a preacher to make things square.
So they sent back East, as was the general rule,
And hired one fresh from divinity school.
When Sunday come, he was all decked out
To preach his sermon, whisper and shout.
But when he stepped out to the podium,
It was all too obvious that no one come.

'Cept one old cowboy in a pew back there,
In his Sunday shirt and his greased-down hair.
He sat there quiet, just watched the floor,
With a 'casional glance toward the church's door.
Time stood still for the longest while
Till the preacher coughed and faked a smile:
"Guess we could try it again next week."
But emotion reigned; he could hardly speak.

His demeanor was that of a scolded pup.
He turned to leave, when ol' Jake spoke up:
"Hold on there, Parson, it ain't your fault,

This story came about from a conversation I had with a cattleman friend, Clair Knudsen of Elko County, Nevada, about feeding cattle the whole load. I put the poem together as a practice in writing meter and rhyme.

173

An' them thar doors ain't like no vault,
'Cause thar ain't locks for to keep folks out;
An' if you don't preach now, Satan's won the bout.
Now, if I was t'haul out a whole load o' hay,
An' only one cow showed, she'd get fed that day."

Well, this preachin' man, in the last few days,
Found it hard to cope with the Western ways.
But he figured as how he'd found his call
From this profound man with his Western drawl.
So he fixed his collar, and he stood up straight
And commenced to expound on the pearly gates;
And he shocked himself at his own recall
Of the book he waved—chapter, verse, and all.

It was God Almighty's omnipotent power
That he lectured on for near an hour,
Then the wages of sin an' Hell's brim fire;
And he didn't weaken, and he didn't tire.
He was jumpin' and screamin' and poundin' the floor,
When he noticed ol' Jake weren't awake anymore.
Now, this made him mad, and he stomped to the pew.
He shook Jake's shoulder and said, "I'm not through.

"You're the one told me 'bout the cow gettin' fed,
An' here you're a-actin' like you're home in bed."
"You're right there, Preach, 'bout the things I told you;
If I'd a load o' hay, it would still stand true:
That cow would get fed, 'tis the cowboy's code—
But I wouldn't feed her the whole durn load."

Waddie Mitchell of Elko, Nevada, was raised as a cowboy and spent 26 years as one. Now signed with Warner Brothers, Mitchell presents the traditions of cowboy poetry and storytelling around the world.

A Coon-Huntin' Story

Jerry Clower

I come from Liberty, Mississippi. Now, as I grew up in that community, the only extracurricular activity we engaged in was going coon huntin' or to revival meeting if we had our crop laid by. That's all we did except work. I want to tell you about one evening when we were going coon huntin' with a pack of hounds.

We hadn't been too busy on this particular day. All we'd done was cut down a few fence rows, shucked and shelled some corn, gone to the mill, drawn up some water because it was wash day, helped get the sow back that had rooted out from under the netwire fence, sharpened two sticks of stove wood real sharp and pegged them down over the bottom wire of the fence so the hogs couldn't root out no more, and had a rat killing. If I'm lying, I'm dying!

Well, after we got through with the rat killing, I walked out on the front porch and hollered, "Hoo, ooh," and them dogs come out from under the house, barking. They knew we was going coon huntin'. I hollered again, and my neighbor way across the sage patch hollered back. That meant "I'll meet you halfway."

We met in the middle of that sage patch, and he had his dogs, Ol' Brummy, Queen, and Spot. I had Tory, Little Red, and Ol' Trailer. We went down into the swamp and started hunting. Oh, we was having such a fine time. Caught four great big ones.

Then I heard a racket, and it scared me, so I whipped around my carbide light that I had wired to my cap, and I started looking in the vicinity of where I'd heard the racket coming from. The beam of light hit a man right in the face, and it like to scared me slap to death because we was hunting on that man's place.

I said, "Mr. Barron, is that you?"

He said, "Yes, Jerry. What are y'all doing?"

"We're hunting."

"How many y'all caught?"

"Four great big ones."

He said, "Well, boys, I'm glad to see you. Y'all want to spend the rest of the evening hunting with me and John?"

Well, I looked, and lo and behold, there was John Eubanks, a man who lived on Mr. Barron's place.

John Eubanks was a professional tree climber. I'm telling you the truth—he didn't believe in shooting no coon out of no tree. It was against his upbringing. He taught us from the day we were born, "Give everything a sporting chance. Whatever you do, give it a sporting chance." He'd have been a great conservationist today if he were here.

John used to say, "Take a crosscut saw coon hunting with you. When you tree a coon, hold the dog, and cut the tree down, or climb the tree, and make the coon jump in amongst the dogs. Give him a sporting chance." A lot of times we'd climb a tree and make a coon jump in amongst 20 dogs, but at least he had the option of whipping all them dogs and walking off if he wanted to. This was strictly left up to the coon.

I said, "Mr. Barron, we'd be glad to go huntin' with you."

He was a rich man, and he had some world-renowned dogs. We hollered three or four times, and they started hunting. We listened. Now, Ol' Brummy didn't bark at nothing but a coon. He had a deep voice, and when you heard him, don't worry about no possums or bobcats— Brummy was running a coon. Ol' Trailer and them famous dogs of Mr. Barron's kept right in there too, and John Eubanks would holler, "Hoo! Speak to him!"

My brother, Sonny, hollered, "Hoo, look for him!"

Oh, it was beautiful. About that time the dogs treed the coon. We rushed down into the swamp, and there the dogs were at the biggest sweet-gum tree in all of the Amite River swamps. It was huge—you couldn't reach around that tree, and there wasn't a limb on it for a long ways up.

I looked at John, and I said, "John, I don't believe you can climb that tree."

That hurt John's feelings. He pooched his lips out, got fighting mad. He said, "There ain't a tree in all these swamps that I can't climb."

He got his brogan shoes off, and he eased up to that sweet-gum tree. He hung his toenails in that bark, and he got his fingernails in it, and he kept easing up the tree, working his way to that bottom limb. He finally got to it and started on up into the branches.

"Knock him out, John!"

John worked his way on up to the top of the tree. Hoo-ooh! What a big one! He reached around in his overalls and got a sharp stick, and he drew back and punched that coon. But it wasn't a coon—it was a lynx! What we called a souped-up wildcat.

That lynx had great big tusks coming out of his mouth and great big claws on the end of his feet, and, people, that thing attacked John up in the top of that tree.

"Whaw! Ooh!" You could hear John squalling.

"What's the matter with John?"

"I don't have no idea what in the world's happening to John."

"Knock him out, John!"

"What in the world's happening to John?"

"Knock him out, John!"

"Wow! Ooh! This thing's killing me!"

The whole top of the tree was shaking. Then the dogs got to biting the bark of the tree and fighting one another, and I kicked 'em and said, "You dogs get away!"

"What's the matter with John?"

"Knock him out, John!"

"Yow-woo! This thing's killing me!"

John knew that Mr. Barron toted a pistol in his belt to shoot snakes with. John kept hollering, "Oh, shoot this thing! Have mercy, this thing's killing me! Shoot this thing!"

Mr. Barron said, "John, I can't shoot up in there. I might hit you."

John said, "Well, just shoot up in here amongst us then. *One* of us has got to have some relief."

Jerry Clower of East Fork, Mississippi, has been named America's best country comic for nine years straight. A former traveling fertilizer salesman, Clower began adding stories to his sales presentations and in 1970 wound up with a record contract. He has 21 best-selling albums on the MCA label.

THE DEBATE IN SIGN LANGUAGE

Syd Lieberman

When people don't have power, many of their tales involve outsmarting those who do. But brains aren't always enough; sometimes you need luck too. This story pleased Jews so much that at least eight versions of it exist. Each variant features debates with different individuals, using different signs. My thanks to Hughes Moir for the signs described in this version.

Once there was an evil king who decided that he wanted to throw all of the Jews out of his country. And the way he planned to go about it was to have a debate with them in sign language.

He said to the Jewish community, "I will give you three signs, and if someone can read my three signs and answer them correctly, you can stay here for the rest of your days. But if not, all of your people will have to go."

Well, the Jewish community was up in arms. No one knew what to do. There were arguments and discussions, and no one wanted to take the responsibility, not even the rabbi. After all, how would they debate a king, let alone do it in sign language?

Finally, after days of arguments back and forth, Yonkel, a little man who sold chickens, said, "Look, if no one else will do it, I will." So they agreed, and off Yonkel went to the debate.

A huge platform had been set up in the center of town, and everybody was gathered around it. The king was on one side, and little Yonkel was on the other.

"Remember," said the king, "I will give you three signs, and if you get them all correct, you and your people can stay in this land. If not, you will have to leave. Here is the first sign."

The king threw an arm into the air and put his hand out, fingers outstretched. Well, Yonkel looked at him and put up a fist in front of his face.

The king said, "Correct! I'm amazed. All right, here is the second sign."

He threw his arm toward Yonkel, with two fingers stretched straight out. Yonkel put one finger in front of his nose.

The king said, "Correct again! Get the third sign right, and all your people will be able to stay."

Then the king reached into the folds of his robe and pulled out a piece of cheese. Little Yonkel looked at him, shrugged, reached into a pouch, and pulled out an egg.

The king said, "Correct again! The Jews can stay."

That night in the castle the whole court gathered around the king. They said to him, "What was that debate about?"

The king said, "It's astonishing that the Jews had a little chicken man who could read my signs. First I put my hand out with my fingers extended to show him that the Jews were scattered all over the world, but he put up his fist to show me that they were one in the hand of God.

"Then I put up two fingers to show him that there were two kings: one in heaven and me, the king on earth. He put up one finger to show me that there was only one king—the king in heaven.

"Finally I brought out a piece of cheese to show him that the Jewish religion had grown old and moldy. But he brought out an egg to show me that it was still fresh and whole. It was truly amazing."

Meanwhile, at Yonkel's everybody had crowded into the chicken store. They said, "What was that debate about?"

Yonkel said, "I don't know. I didn't even know it had started. I mean, he reached out to grab me, so I put up my fist to show him that I would punch him if he touched me.

"Then he put out two fingers to poke my eyes out. So I put up one to block them.

"By then I guess he knew I was going to stand up to him. So he brought out his lunch, and I brought out mine."

Syd Lieberman of Evanston, Illinois, is a storyteller and a teacher. He spins many kinds of yarns but specializes in Jewish material, family and historical stories, and ghost tales. The American Library Association has given three of his story audiotapes Notable Children's Recording awards, and the Parents' Choice Foundation has honored a fourth.

The $50,000 Racehorse

Hannah McConnell Gillenwater

When I was a girl, I was my dad's shadow. Everywhere he went, I tagged right along. One of my favorite places to go was John Mauk's country store in Stony Point, Tennessee.

I remember that store's screen door and how the hinges would squeak. John kept those old wood floors oiled, and I can still recall the smell. That was *the* store in Stony Point, complete with a pot-bellied stove. All the gentlemen would sit around that stove, especially when the weather turned cold. They'd put a fire in the stove, and it'd be red-hot at the bottom. They'd sit there, chewin' and spittin'. I'd sit there too and listen to the stories they had to tell.

Now, John Mauk was quite a character. Long before I was even a gleam in my daddy's eye, they say that John was probably the meanest man in Hawkins County. He never would go to Sunday school, church, or revival meetings—in fact, he'd cheat you blind. He'd charge you a little more than he should and keep his finger on the scales when he weighed out fruit or vegetables. He was a pretty ornery fellow.

Well, John was getting up in years, and the people in the community were starting to worry about his soul and what would happen to him in the hereafter. There happened to be a traveling Baptist revival coming through Hawkins County, and some of the little old ladies down at the Baptist church commenced to prayin' for old John. They started tellin' him, "John, you need to come to this revival." Well, they hounded him, and the men of the church hounded him too, until finally he said, "All right, I'll come."

It was on the last night of the revival that John Mauk came, and he got religion. He said, "I've turned over a new leaf. From here on out, I'm going to be living at the foot of the cross." He got such a good case of religion that afterward, every time he went to ring up a sale in his store, he'd quote a verse of Scripture.

Well, this particular day in October—the sun was shinin' down, but there was a definite nip in the air—we were all sittin' around the stove in John's store, and I was listening to stories and wantin' a chew of tobacco, but they wouldn't let me have one. And in the door came this little girl.

John said, "Well, howdy, honey. What can I do for you today?" She said, "I want some candy." So John handed the big old glass candy jar down to her, and she filled her pockets full, gave him her money, and left. She must have gotten 15 cents' worth of candy for a nickel. We couldn't believe that he'd been so kind to that kid. Old John never had liked younguns much.

He went around to the cash register and looked up into the heavens. Then he rang up the sale, and he said, "Suffer the little children to come unto me."

About 10 minutes later Cougar Myers's mama came in there, hunting a birthday present for her daddy. John let her come around behind the counter, and he showed her the bandana handkerchiefs and the pocket combs and the sock supporters and the Barlow knives and Aqua Velva and stuff. She picked her out a nice present for old man Myers, and John gift-wrapped it for her for free with some old Christmas paper he had left over.

She paid him and went out the door, and as he went to the register to ring up the sale, he looked heavenward again and said, "Honor thy father and thy mother."

Boy, by then, we were impressed with all that Scripture. It wasn't long afterward that we heard a big commotion outside the store. We looked out, and a brand-new bright blue pickup truck with a matching horse trailer had pulled up in front of the store. It had out-of-the-county license tags. Nobody knew that old feller.

Sure enough, he got out of the truck and came into the store. He had on a sheepskin coat, a big old 10-gallon hat, and pointy cowboy boots. He came a-struttin' in, walked up to the counter, and growled, "I want to buy me a horse blanket."

John said, "I'll see what I got." So he went to the back room, and he had three horse blankets there. They were all the very same kind, but each one was a different color. Naturally, John got the top one off the shelf and brought it out and laid it on the counter. The man said, "All right, how much is that?"

John said, "Sir, that'll be $9.95."

That man yelled, "Nine ninety-five? Nine ninety-five? Buddy, I've got a $50,000 racehorse in that trailer out there, and I'm not about to put a cheap blanket like that on my horse! You can just forget it if you haven't got anything better."

Old John said, "You want a better blanket."

The man said, "Yeah, I want a better blanket."

John went to the back room again and took the next one down the line—same thing, just a different color—and brought it out and put it down on the counter. The man said, "All right, how much is that one?"

John said, "Sir, that'll be $19.95."

The man said, "Buddy, I thought I *told* you I had a $50,000 racehorse out there, and no cheap stuff like that is going on the back of my horse!"

John said, "Sir, I aim to please. I think I got another one. I know what you want now."

So John took back that horse blanket and brought out the last one, carrying it as if it were some royal gem, and he laid it down real gentle in front of that man. Old John turned back one corner of the blanket, rubbing his hand over it, and he said, "Now, how is this?"

The man said, "How much is that one?"

John said, "Sir, that's the best blanket in the house. That'll be $99.95."

The man said, "I'll take it." He whipped out the fattest wallet I've ever seen. Now, it might have been filled mostly with ones—I don't know. But he thumbed through there and pulled out a crisp $100 bill and laid it on the counter. He stuck that blanket under his arm and said, "Keep the change." Then he went out that squeaky screen door, jumped into his pickup truck, and took off.

There was dead silence. We couldn't believe what had just transpired. John stood behind the counter, holding that hundred-dollar bill in his hands. He looked over at us, and we looked at him. He waited. We reckoned he was waiting for some divine inspiration.

Finally he went over to the cash register. He looked toward heaven, rang that sale up, and said, "He was a stranger, and I took him in."

Hannah McConnell Gillenwater learned stories from Southwest Virginia and the East Tennessee hills from her parents and both sets of grandparents. She tells stories and teaches reading to fifth- through eighth-grade students and encourages them to collect and tell their own tales. Gillenwater lives in Rogersville, Tennessee.

THE LIONMAKERS

Nancy Schimmel

I thought of this tale from the Panchatantra (an eighth-century anthology created for the enlightenment of a king's son) when I was asked to find some old stories that relate to modern problems—like our relationship with technology. Another teller I know told a version of it for the Ohio Atomic Energy Commission.

Four men grew up together in a little village in India. Three of the men were scholars, but the fourth man never studied anything. In fact, he never read a book in his life. He just got along as best he could on his own common sense. But the four men had been friends as children, and they remained friends despite their differences.

One day the four friends were sitting under the trees, talking of this and that, when one of the scholars said, "Something has been bothering me. I have spent all my life studying, and I know many things, but I know them only from books. I don't know if my knowledge works out in the world."

"You know," said another of the scholars, "the same thing has been bothering me! But somehow this little village doesn't seem to offer sufficient scope for me to try out my vast knowledge."

"Clearly," said the third scholar, "we must venture into the world and try out our knowledge there." The three scholars agreed, but then there was their friend to consider. They had always done everything together, share and share alike, but suppose—suppose they found some lost treasure by using their knowledge? Suppose they solved a problem for a rajah, and he rewarded them with gold and jewels?

For years the three of them had studied late into the night to prepare themselves for their work, and their friend had done nothing. He had only his common sense, and what rajah would be impressed with that? They argued the matter back and forth as they so enjoyed doing, but finally they decided to do as they had always done: share and share alike.

So the four of them started on their journey. For many days they walked along, until one day they saw some bones scattered by the path. One of the scholars said, "I can tell from my studies that these bones are those of a lion. Now, it happens that I have learned how to arrange the bones as they would be in a living lion."

"Really?" said the second scholar. "That is interesting—for it happens that from my studies I know how to clothe the bones with flesh and blood and skin and fur."

"Indeed?" said the third scholar. "How curious. It happens that I know how to perform the next step. Once the animal is formed, I know how to breathe the breath of life into it. Clearly this is the place where we should try out our knowledge to see if it works in the world." The other scholars agreed.

The fourth man, the one who wasn't a scholar, was simply struck dumb by this display of learning and said nothing at all.

So the first scholar stepped forward and arranged the bones as they would be in a living lion. Then he stepped back, and the second scholar stepped forward and clothed the bones with flesh and blood and skin and fur. Then he stepped back, and the third scholar stepped forward to breathe the breath of life into the animal, when the fourth man said, "Wait! That's a lion you're about to bring to life. It could eat us up. Stop and think about what you're doing!"

"We know what we're doing," said the scholars. "We have studied this sort of thing all our lives. Don't worry. Just leave everything to us."

"Well, all right," said their friend, "but could you wait till I climb a tree?"

"Certainly," said the scholars, and they waited till their friend had climbed a tree that was close at hand. Then the third scholar went back to the procedure of breathing the breath of life into the animal. Sure enough, the lion started breathing, opened its eyes, looked at the three scholars, sprang upon them, and ate them up.

After the lion had gone away, the fourth man, the one who wasn't a scholar, climbed down from the tree and made his way back to the village, taking with him no great treasure of gold and jewels but only his own good common sense.

Nancy Schimmel is a storyteller and songwriter based in Berkeley, California, where she occasionally writes songs on local issues and sings them for the city council. She performs this story on Tell Me a Story: Nancy Schimmel *(Kartes Video, 1986), but she'd rather you tell it yourself than watch her do it.*

Huntin' Werewolf
For Papa Keel

Bob Jenkins

My great granddaddy was a farmer, and everyone down in Pamlico County, North Carolina, called him Papa Keel. I loved Papa 'cause he treated me like a grown-up, and he taught me all the manly things—how to track game through the woods, which plants were safe to eat, and which ones would kill you.

But the day come when I had to prove my manhood to Papa. You see, the woods around them parts had strange things goin' on: we had been infected with a blight of supernatural *phenomen-eye*.

Late one night we heard a blood-freezin' howl from the barn. We went out for a look. One of the newborn lambs was missing. Behind the barn, in the light of the full moon, we found footprints in the soft ground—big footprints, big ol' monster footprints.

It was the werewolf!

Papa Keel looks me right in the eye and says, "Bobby boy, today's the day you prove you're a man. Go out and find that no-good shape-shifter, kill it, and bring it home for supper." Then he took his old single-shot .22-caliber rifle down from its peg and dug around in a box till he come up with a .22-caliber silver bullet.

"But where do I find the monster?" says I.

"If I put your brains in a jaybird, he'd fly backwards. Go pick up the tracks in the soft ground, and keep following them tracks till you come to the very last pair of them tracks, and you'll see a werewolf standing in 'em. Shoot him, and bring him back for soup meat!"

I loaded up the silver bullet and set off, stepping high and proud like a rooster in deep mud.

I followed the tracks, came out of a patch of woods, and there on the other side of a cow pasture was that hairy ol' wolfman, bending over and munching on something nasty.

Well, I could shoot that rifle with the best of 'em, but the werewolf was still too far away for a good clean shot, so I commenced to sneak up on him.

For as long as anyone can remember, my great-grandfather Harley T. Keel was called Papa. Tall, slim, and weathered, with snow-white hair brushed straight back from his wide brow, Papa Keel was the old man of Pamlico County, North Carolina. He was my boyhood idol and my grown-up ideal—a great Southern gentleman.

189

Now, listen up, city folk—there are two ways to sneak across a cow pasture: the wrong way and the right way. The wrong way is to look ahead where you're going. The right way is to look down at what you're about to step in. I took the wrong way and stepped in something real slickery. My feet went out from under me, I landed flat on my backside, and the rifle discharged straight up in the air. Folks, it must have been a million-to-one chance, but that silver bullet streaked straight up through a whole flock of vampire bats that were flying by and knocked down about a dozen of 'em.

Vampire bats were falling every which way, screeching and flapping to beat all. Well, the commotion scared that werewolf away, but Papa Keel would just as soon eat crispy-fried vampire bat as some smelly werewolf, wouldn't you?

So I was hopping around, picking up vampire bats and stuffin' 'em into my pockets, when I heard this horrible roar.

I looked up, and charging out of the woods was this awful-looking Thing. It was horrible. How horrible was it? It was so horrible it could squat behind a pine tree and hatch a monkey. I don't even want to describe it, but heck, you've paid enough for this slick book, so I will. The Thing had a body like a lion and eagle wings growing out of its back. It had the face of a woman and a great big mouth full of teeth.

It was a sphinx monster! And it was coming after me!

I turned to run the other way, and there, coming out of the woods on the other side, was another monster. This one was a tall green creature made up of different human body parts all sewed and bolted together.

It was a Frankenstein!

I was caught between them two monsters. The sphinx reached me first, its mouth wide open. I didn't know what to do—so I stuck my arm down its throat. Now, that surprised it, but it had that whatchamacallit, *momentum*, and it just kept coming up my arm. It kept coming, and I kept pushing till my hand popped out its other end.

Now, that really surprised it.

So it started to back up real fast. I just grabbed on real tight and pulled. Folks, I snatched that sucker inside out.

Ree-pulsive!

Old inside-out sphinx monster went galumphing off through the woods, blood and guts flying every which way. But I didn't have time to savor my triumph 'cause just then Frankenstein reached me and put them big green hands around my throat.

"I'm gonna twist your head around so far, you can scratch the back of your neck with your front teeth!" says Frankenstein.

I had to think fast.

"Okay," says I, "if nothing but a killing will satisfy you, can't I please say my prayers?"

"Cut 'em short," says Frankie, "'cause I'm gonna eat you up."

So I kneel down and commence to pray. "O Lord, Thou knowest that when I killed Count Dracula and Dr. Jekyll and Mr. Hyde that I did it in self-defense. Thou knowest, O Lord, that when I cut the heart out of Godzilla and strewed the brains of Jack the Ripper upon the ground that it was forced upon me. And now, O Lord, I must put this miserable green critter back into his coffin. O Lord, have mercy on his soul."

Then I get up off my knees and roll up my sleeves real reluctantly, and ol' Frankie is just standing there, scared half to death and a-shakin' all over like a wet dog. Folks, he was shakin' so hard that little body parts were falling off of him—ears, fingers, nuts, and bolts.

I reached down and picked up one of the bolts and put it in my pocket to keep as evidence that it all really happened. Now, where is it? I had it just the other day . . . You'll have to trust me on that one.

Frankenstein looked so sorrowful, it just about broke my heart. So I patted ol' Frankie on the shoulder and give him my hankie to blow his nose. He looked down at me just like a little puppy, and I knowed I made a friend for life.

Me and Frankenstein shook hands and sat down on a log to chew a little fat and dip a little snuff. Now, let me tell you folks something— Frankenstein ain't one of your little "pinch between cheek and gum" snuffers. Frankenstein is a flat-out, low-slung, bottom-lipful dipper.

So we was just sittin' there, mindin' our own business, when all of a sudden a big shadow falls over us. We turn around, and right there, rising up out of the grass is that ol' werewolf. He starts comin' at us real slow-like and a-grinnin' like a baked possum.

Folks, them werewolf critters has fangs as big as a rattlesnake, and when they bite you, first you turn blue, then you turn yellow, then all your hair falls out and your fingernails fall off, and you're dead as a doornail before you can take two steps.

The only known werewolf antidote is sour-mash whiskey, which is why you find so many drunks in that part of North Carolina, just keepin' werewolves away. But me and Frankie didn't have no whiskey.

What we did have was one knock-down-drag-out do-jigger of a hand-to-hand combat with dirty death. We rassled and punched and clawed and kicked and scratched and bit, but it weren't no use. Me and Frankie was gettin' whupped. Just for a second I got that wolfman's arms pinned down, and I yelled, "Run for it, Frankie! Save yourself!"

Sure enough, Frankenstein got clean away. As for me?

Well, as for me. That werewolf bit me all over my body, and I turned blue, then I turned yellow, then my hair fell out and my fingernails fell off, and it killed me and ate me. Yep, it gobbled me up.

Folks, I don't blame you if you think this is a tall tale. And I know you admire a man who will tell the truth under any and all circumstances, but don't you just hate a liar?

Bob Jenkins of Los Gatos, California, has been telling stories to audiences for more than 25 years. He has performed all over the United States, in Asia, and in the South Pacific. Many of his tales are set in the Croatan Swamp of North Carolina and revolve around his great-grandfather Papa Keel.

THE BRAVE LITTLE PARROT

Rafe Martin

This is my retelling of a 2,500-year-old Buddhist tale, whose message seems entirely contemporary. Our world is burning, and each of us can help do something about it. Small deeds, done wholeheartedly, may have the potential to change everything— in ways we might never guess. For many of us, telling stories is such a way. Fly on, little parrot!

Once a little parrot lived happily in a beautiful forest. But one day without warning, lightning flashed, thunder crashed, and a dead tree burst into flames. Sparks, carried on the rising wind, began to leap from branch to branch and tree to tree.

The little parrot smelled the smoke. "Fire!" she cried. "Run to the river!" Flapping her wings, rising higher and higher, she flew toward the safety of the river's far shore. After all, she was a bird and could fly away.

But as she flew, she could see that many animals were already surrounded by the flames and could not escape. Suddenly a desperate idea, a way to save them, came to her.

Darting to the river, she dipped herself in the water. Then she flew back over the now-raging fire. Thick smoke coiled up, filling the sky. Walls of flame shot up, now on one side, now on the other. Pillars of fire leapt before her. Twisting and turning through a mad maze of flame, the little parrot flew bravely on.

Having reached the heart of the burning forest, the little parrot shook her wings. And the few tiny drops of water that still clung to her feathers tumbled like jewels down into the flames and vanished with a hiss.

Then the little parrot flew back through the flames and smoke to the river. Once more she dipped herself in the cool water and flew back over the burning forest. Once more she shook her wings, and a few drops of water tumbled like jewels into the flames. *Hisssss.*

Back and forth she flew, time and time again from the river to the forest, from the forest to the river. Her feathers became charred. Her feet and claws were scorched. Her lungs ached. Her eyes burned. Her mind spun as dizzily as a spinning spark. Still the little parrot flew on.

At that moment some of the blissful gods floating overhead in their cloud palaces of ivory and gold happened to look down and see the

194

little parrot flying among the flames. They pointed at her with their perfect hands. Between mouthfuls of honied foods, they exclaimed, "Look at that foolish bird! She's trying to put out a raging forest fire with a few sprinkles of water! How absurd!" They laughed.

But one of those gods, strangely moved, changed himself into a golden eagle and flew down, down toward the little parrot's fiery path.

The little parrot was just nearing the flames again, when a great eagle with eyes like molten gold appeared at her side. "Go back, little bird!" said the eagle in a solemn and majestic voice. "Your task is hopeless. A few drops of water can't put out a forest fire. Cease now, and save yourself before it is too late."

But the little parrot continued to fly on through the smoke and flames. She could hear the great eagle flying above her as the heat grew fiercer. He called out, "Stop, foolish little parrot! Stop! Save yourself!

"I didn't need some great, shining eagle," coughed the little parrot, "to tell me that. My own mother, the dear bird, could have told me the same thing long ago. Advice! I don't need advice. I just"—cough, cough—"need someone to help!"

Rising higher, the eagle, who was a god, watched the little parrot flying through the flames. High above he could see his own kind, those carefree gods, still laughing and talking even as many animals cried out in pain and fear far below. He grew ashamed of the gods' carefree life, and a single desire was kindled in his heart.

"God though I am," he exclaimed, "how I wish I could be just like that little parrot. Flying on, brave and alone, risking all to help—what a rare and marvelous thing! What a wonderful little bird!"

Moved by these new feelings, the great eagle began to weep. Stream after stream of sparkling tears began pouring from his eyes. Wave upon wave they fell, washing down like a torrent of rain upon the fire, upon the forest, upon the animals and the little parrot herself.

Where those cooling tears fell, the flames shrank down and died. Smoke still curled up from the scorched earth, yet new life was already boldly pushing forth—shoots, stems, blossoms, and leaves. Green grass sprang up from among the still-glowing cinders.

Where the eagle's teardrops sparkled on the little parrot's wings, new feathers now grew: red feathers, green feathers, yellow feathers too. Such bright colors! Such a pretty bird!

The animals looked at one another in amazement. They were whole and well. Not one had been harmed. Up above in the clear blue sky they could see their brave friend, the little parrot, looping and soaring in delight. When all hope was gone, somehow she had saved them.

"Hurray!" they cried. "Hurray for the brave little parrot and for this sudden, miraculous rain!"

Rafe Martin of Rochester, New York, is an award-winning author and storyteller whose books and tapes have received awards from both the American Library Association and the Parents' Choice Foundation. His book The Hungry Tigress: Buddhist Legends and Jataka Tales *(Parallax Press, 1990) received a 1992 Anne Izard Storyteller's Choice Award. Martin has been a featured storyteller, speaker, and teacher at festivals, conferences, schools, museums, and libraries throughout the United States and abroad.*

Br'er Rabbit Builds a Home

Jackie Torrence

Once all the critters in the big wood decided they should go in together and build themselves a house. Br'er Possum, Br'er Bear, Br'er Coon, Br'er Wolf, and even Br'er Rabbit. All of them took different jobs.

Br'er Rabbit said that he would have to do something on the ground because he couldn't climb ladders—he said that made him dizzy in the head. He couldn't work outside because the sun made him shiver. So he got himself a pencil and a ruler, and he started measuring and marking and marking and measuring. He went in and out and out and in and all around and up and down, and he was so busy that all the other critters thought he was putting down a whole passel of work. Yet all the time he was doing absolutely nothing.

Now, the critters that was working was *really* working. They built a fine house, the likes of which nobody in them parts had ever seen. Plenty rooms upstairs, plenty rooms downstairs. They put a whole heap of chimneys, fireplaces, and a lot of other wonderful things in their house.

After the house was finished, each critter picked a room. Old Br'er Rabbit picked one of the upstairs rooms and proceeded to furnish it. While all the other critters were busy furnishing their rooms, Br'er Rabbit was sneaking into his room a shotgun, a big black cannon, and a huge tub of water.

When everything was all finished, the critters cooked a big supper in celebration of their new home. After supper everybody took seats in the parlor. Everybody was laughing and talking and having a good time. Br'er Rabbit sat there for a little while, and then all of a sudden he commenced to yawning and stretching and yawning and stretching, and after a while longer he excused himself for bed.

Well, the other critters just stayed on and laughed and talked and had a good old time in their parlor. While they were talking and laughing, old Br'er Rabbit stuck his head through his room door and

This story happens to be the answer to a question I asked my grandpa when I was 4 years old. "Where does Br'er Rabbit live?" I said. He never gave a straight answer but always told a tale. This story is the answer I received.

yelled out, "When a big fellow like me wants to sit down, whereabouts do you think he ought to sit?"

All the other critters laughed, and they hollered up the steps, "When a big fellow like you can't sit in a chair, he'd better sit on the floor."

"Then watch out down there," said Br'er Rabbit. "I'm fixing to sit right now." And about that time Br'er Rabbit pulled the trigger on his shotgun. *Kerbloom!* went the gun.

Well, all the other critters looked at one another and wondered what in the world that was. Everything was quiet—nobody said anything for a long time.

But after a while they forgot the noise and started talking and laughing again. As soon as that happened, old Br'er Rabbit stuck his head through his door again and yelled, "When a big fellow like me wants to sneeze, whereabouts can he sneeze?"

The other critters looked at one another, and then they hollered up the stairs, "When a big fellow like you can't hold a sneeze, he sneezes where he pleases!"

"Then watch out down there, 'cause I'm gonna sneeze right here," said Br'er Rabbit. And he lit the fuse on his cannon. *Boom!*

Well, the sound of the cannon knocked the critters out of their chairs, the glass shook in the windows, the dishes rattled in the cupboard, and old Br'er Bear hit the floor right on his bottom. "Lordy be," said old Br'er Bear, "I think old Br'er Rabbit's got a powerful bad cold. I think I'll just step outside for a breath of fresh air."

After a bit all the other critters settled down. They felt a little uneasy, but they kept talking and laughing till all at once Br'er Rabbit stuck his head out his door again and yelled, "When a big fellow like me wants to take a chew of tobacco, whereabouts is he supposed to spit?"

The other critters looked at one another, feeling kind of mad, and they hollered up the steps, "If you be a big man or a little man, spit where you please!"

"Then look out down there," yelled Br'er Rabbit. "I'm a-gonna spit." About that time he turned over that tub of water, and the water came rolling down the steps. *Kersplash!*

Well, every one of the critters heard it coming, and they lit out in all different directions. Some jumped out the windows. Some bolted through the doors. Everybody cleared that house but fast.

Old Br'er Rabbit watched them as they tore off in different directions through the woods. Then he locked the doors, closed the windows, went to bed, and slept like he owned the world.

If the others didn't want to live in their brand-new house, and if they'd run off scared, it wasn't *his* fault. Br'er Rabbit slept in peace.

And that's the end of that.

Jackie Torrence of Salisbury, North Carolina, has been a storyteller for 20 years. One of America's most respected tellers, she has traveled through every state in the union except South Dakota. Torrence recently received an honorary doctoral degree from Livingstone College in Salisbury.

THE RED LION

Diane Wolkstein

This ancient Persian tale about confronting one's fears is a compelling story to tell for listeners of all ages. Whatever our age, we all live with fears of different kinds. As the years have passed, with the telling of this story, I've begun to view my never-ending cycle of fears as challenges rather than threats— opportunities leading to greater understanding.

When the king of Persia died, there was great weeping, for he had been a brave and wise leader. Yet in little more than a month the mourning would be over, and the king's son would be crowned. But before the prince could be crowned, he would have to prove his courage, just as every prince before him had done, by fighting the Red Lion.

One day during this time the vizier went to the young prince and urged him to prepare himself for the contest. The prince trembled. He had always been afraid of lions, and the Red Lion was the most ferocious of lions. So the prince decided to run away.

That night when it was very dark, he crept out of his bedroom, mounted his horse, and rode off. He rode two days and nights. On the morning of the third day he entered a grove of trees and heard a sweet melody. Dismounting, he walked quietly until he saw a shepherd, sitting in a clearing and playing a flute. All about the shepherd the sheep stood listening.

"God be with you," said the shepherd to the stranger.

"And with you," the prince replied, "but please do not stop your song."

The shepherd took up his flute and played for the clouds, for the winds, for his sheep, and for the stranger.

When he finished, the prince spoke: "Surely you are wondering who I am. I wish I could tell you my name. But it is a secret that must stay locked in my heart. I beg you to believe me; I am no enemy. I am an honorable youth who has been forced to flee from his home."

"You are welcome to stay with me," the shepherd answered. "I would be glad of your company, and I can show you a place that will cause you to forget your troubles."

Hour after hour the prince and the shepherd walked, the prince leading his horse and the sheep following behind the shepherd. As the sun was setting, they came to the most beautiful valley the prince had ever seen. It was perfectly quiet, and the prince and the shepherd sat and gazed in wonder at the hills in front of them. Suddenly the shepherd jumped up.

"Time to go!" he said.

"But why must we leave so quickly?" asked the prince. "Can there be any place on earth more lovely?"

"It is beautiful," the shepherd agreed. And then he raised his sleeve, revealing a long, cruel red scar. He traced his finger along the scar and said, "Lions! Once I was late returning to the village, and the village gates were closed. This is the result. I do not want it to happen a second time."

"Please return to the village with the sheep," the prince said. "I cannot go with you." He mounted his horse and rode north. He rode two days and nights, and on the third morning he came to a desert.

He and his horse were tired and hungry and thirsty, and the wind blew sand in the prince's face. Suddenly his horse neighed. Through the streaming sands he saw the tents of an Arab camp. His horse began to prance, but the prince pulled back on the bridle and continued to ride slowly to show that his was a peaceful visit.

An Arab sheik greeted him with courtesy. He offered the prince food and made sure his horse was fed and cared for. After the prince had eaten, he said to the sheik, "Forgive me if I do not reveal my name. Because of certain troubles it is a secret that must stay locked in my heart. But I have jewels and precious stones I would gladly give you if you would allow me to remain with you."

"You are our guest," the sheik replied, and he refused to accept any of the prince's treasures.

The following morning the sheik provided the prince with a magnificent stallion, and for the next three days the prince rode with the sheik and his companions, hunting antelope.

On the third evening the sheik spoke to the prince. "My men are pleased with your spirit," he said, "and with your skill at hunting. But there will soon be a battle. My men want to know if they can rely on your strength and courage. To the south lies a range of hills known as the Red Hills. It is lion country. Ride there tomorrow on the stallion. Take your sword and spear, and bring us back the hide of a lion to show us we can count on you on the day of battle."

That night when it was very still, the prince slipped out of his tent. He stroked the beloved stallion he had ridden and whispered goodbye in his ear. Then he mounted his own horse and rode west.

After two days and nights he came to a country of rolling meadows and green fields. There in the distance he saw a splendid red sandstone palace. At the gates the prince took off his ring and asked the guard to present it to the emir. Immediately the prince was invited to enter the palace.

As he was explaining his situation to the emir, Perizide, the emir's daughter, appeared. The emir, who was impressed with the prince's good manners and fine speech, said to his daughter, "My child, please show this young man our palace and gardens, and invite him to the entertainment this evening."

Perizide led the prince through room after room and then out to the garden, where flowers and trees of every kind grew. In the middle of the garden was an oval pool filled with rose water, and in the water floated a lily. It was perfect—and yet not as beautiful as Perizide.

After dinner in the cool evening air, Perizide provided the entertainment, playing the lute and singing. As the prince listened, he felt his soul rising higher and higher. *This is why I have run away,* he thought, *so I might find Perizide.*

"Rrraaagggh!"

"What was that?" cried the prince, jumping to his feet.

"Oh, that's just our guard Boulak. He's yawning."

"Yawning?" repeated the prince.

"Yes," said Perizide. "He does that when it is late. I will say goodnight now."

After she left, the emir stood up. "It is late for me too. Come. I will show you to your bedroom."

They had just begun to climb the staircase when the prince looked up. His hand froze on the banister. There at the top of the landing stood an enormous lion.

"Oh, that's just Boulak," said the emir. "He's perfectly harmless. He never attacks unless someone is afraid of him."

"Oh, I'm not, ah, quite r-r-eady for, ah, s-s-sleep," stammered the prince.

"Well, then, come up when you wish," said the emir. "Yours is the first room on the right."

The prince backed down the stairs. He backed down the corridor, into the music room, and locked the doors. He sat on a chair and waited. Soon he heard the lion padding down the stairs. He heard him claw at the door. The door shook. The lion roared: "Rrraaagggh!"

The prince thought the lion would tear down the door and devour him, but he just sat there. He did not try to run away. The lion roared again: "Rrraaagggh!"

The prince listened. The lion roared a third time. Suddenly the prince realized that the roars were not threats—they were warnings. They were telling him, "Three times you have run away. If you run away again—wherever you may go—a lion will be waiting." A lion would always be waiting for the prince until he went home to fight his own lion.

The prince listened. Boulak did not roar again. Then the prince heard the lion padding back up the stairs.

Early the next morning the prince explained that he had to return home at once. He mounted his horse and, thinking only of the Red Lion, rode day and night until he reached the palace.

At the appointed time the prince entered the crowded arena. The emir, Perizide, the sheik, and the shepherd were all there, seated in the stands. But the prince did not look up. No, his eyes were on the doors from which the Red Lion would emerge. He waited.

The doors opened. The lion sprang out. The prince stood firm, his spear in his hand. The lion roared and leapt—right over the prince's head. When the prince whirled around to throw his spear, he saw the Red Lion lying on his back, waving his paws in the air like a playful puppy. Then the lion trotted up to him and affectionately licked his hands.

The Red Lion was tame. Every lion that had ever fought a prince of Persia had been tame—only fear would make him ferocious.

So the prince was crowned king of Persia. In due time he married Perizide, and the two lived together happily and ruled their kingdom wisely and well.

Diane Wolkstein of New York City has been telling stories for more than 25 years. She is the creator of 10 audiotapes and a videotape; the author of 18 books, including The First Love Stories *(Harper Collins, 1991); and a co-founder of Cloudstone, a multimedia publishing company. Wolkstein gives storytelling workshops throughout the United States and teaches storytelling at the Bank Street College of Education in New York.*

Rainy Weather

Donald Davis

Uncle Frank was a fox hunter. Although he knew about fishing and squirrel hunting and coon hunting and all the rest, the sport of his life was fox hunting.

Many a night I left home with him before dark, a passel of foxhounds with us, to head up to a little building he had built on the peak of the ridge between Jolly Cove and the Crawfords' land.

On the outside wall of this small camping shelter built of framing timber and canvas was a large hand-lettered sign: World Headquarters, Greater Iron Duff Fox Hunters' Association, Frank M. Davis, Fox-Pro.

Uncle Frank was not the founder of the Greater Iron Duff Fox Hunters' Association. Their tradition was much longer even than his fox-hunting life. In those days, though, he was their leader: always an officer, always present, and of course, the one on whose farm the headquarters was located.

Fox hunting in the Southern mountains is not a violent sport. It isn't even a sport in which human beings are involved in the pursuit. Southern fox hunting is a subtle sport of listening. It is, perhaps, more akin to music appreciation than to most other forms of hunting, in which the kill is the goal.

Once the hunters were installed in the open-sided headquarters building, Uncle Frank would let the dogs loose. They would circle and sniff until they picked up a trail and then set off, singing their barking songs in pursuit of the fox.

The point was not to catch the fox. The dogs' interest was in staying on the trail. The human hunters' interest was in listening to them sing as they did so.

Uncle Frank knew each hound by voice. "There goes Old Belle," he would say, indicating a rapidly yelping dog off in the cove. "She must be running in the wet ground. She's got the longest toenails, and

My Uncle Frank had a variety of foxhounds, and he was often asked what had become of a particular dog. One time he answered that the dog in question had trailed a fox all the way to Baltimore and been found barking at a fur coat. My memory of that explanation was the seed for this story.

she can always outrun the rest of them on wet ground.

"Over there's Warbler," he would say, indicating a dog who almost yodeled when he barked. "You'd never miss old Warbler!"

And so the night would go on—with, of course, a full bacon-and-egg midnight snack—as we listened to the dogs run and sing, lose the trail, pick it up, and run and sing again until they were worn out. Then we'd snooze a little before going back to the house.

One night I said to Uncle Frank, "I'd like to be a real dog-owning fox hunter when I grow up, Uncle Frank—not just a visitor."

"Well, son," he replied, "you can't just decide to do that."

"Why? Why can't I be a fox hunter?"

He cleared the matter up. "You may get to be a fox hunter, son. But you can't decide to be one. You see, fox hunting's a vocation. You have to have a calling to be a real fox hunter."

"Well, I'll be called then. How do I get called?" I asked, determined to be a fox hunter.

"Oh, that's not too hard." Uncle Frank's eyes were sparkling. "There are a lot of ways to be called. Why, one member of this club, who shall remain unnamed, was driving home from work one day when he started thinking about his wife, whom he was going home to. At that very moment he got the call to fox hunt. There's lots of ways to get the call.

"The clearest call, I think, is heard by those who love the music of nature so much that they just can't resist the song of those dogs on the trail of a fox. Listen to the music, son, and there's a good chance that you will get the call."

One of Uncle Frank's responsibilities as a perpetual officer of the Greater Iron Duff Fox Hunters' Association was to travel each year to the Pine Barrens of New Jersey for the National Foxhound Championship. He and one other officer of the club (usually Cousin

Tom, since he had retired from the post office) would take Iron Duff's finest foxhound and enter him in the contest.

There in New Jersey amid the cranberry bogs those great foxhounds, gathered from across the nation, would run in competition against one another. At the end of the three-day contest, two dogs would be crowned Mister and Miz Foxhound U.S.A. This was the highest honor that could come to any foxhound in America.

During this particular year Uncle Frank and Cousin Tom headed north for New Jersey with Old Belle, the dog with the long toenails. They figured those long toenails might give her an advantage in the country around the cranberry bogs.

Belle ran well, but she did not win. Uncle Frank and Tom were not too disappointed, though, because something else had captured their attention: the special featured guest of the competition.

Fishhook, an ancient dog, long senile and run-down, was the foxhound Grand Marshal of Honor. The honor was his because he had been crowned Mister Foxhound U.S.A. seven years in a row—more times than any other dog in history.

Twenty-one years old now, Fishhook could no longer stand up, but he was comfortably nestled in a polished walnut dog bed on a Sealy Posturepedic mattress made up with gold satin sheets. There was a little gold pillow under his chin to hold his head up, and there were six young lady dogs assigned to wait on him and make sure that he had everything he needed. Fishhook was a hound with a glorious past.

Uncle Frank and Cousin Tom looked him over, saw all his medals and ribbons, and read about his glorious past. That night at their campsite Uncle Frank and Cousin Tom got to talking about Fishhook. "Do you know what, Frank?" Tom said. "My boy's in school down in Raleigh at State College, you know . . . "

"I know," Uncle Frank replied. "What do they call that subject he's studying? Something about taking care of animals, isn't it?"

"Animal husbandry is what they call it," Tom said. "That's what I've been thinking about. Every time he comes home from Raleigh, he tells me about all the modern miracles of animal medical science. Why, one of these days they're going to make a pig that's nothing but bacon and ham and a chicken that lays two or three eggs a day!"

"I've read about some of that stuff," Uncle Frank put in. "I even hear some feller's working on an electric rooster. But what got you to thinking about it now, Tom?"

"Fishhook," Tom replied, almost in a whisper. "What I'm thinking is that you and I could buy that old dog—probably pretty cheap since he's got so much mileage on him—and my boy could restore him. I figure that even if his legs are shot, we could build him enough to breed him. We could introduce an entirely new bloodline into the Iron Duff foxhounds."

Uncle Frank, who had had the very same notion himself, thought that was a fine idea. The two of them decided to give it a try.

The next day they approached Fishhook's owner. There was nothing to it. The man had nursed the old dog all the way from Kentucky to the Pine Barrens of New Jersey, and he didn't figure Fishhook would live to make the trip back home again. He didn't really believe the dog would make it back to Iron Duff, North Carolina, with Uncle Frank and Cousin Tom either. He threw in the walnut dog bed for good measure.

It was a slow and careful trip back home, but with plenty of rest stops, Uncle Frank and Cousin Tom made it just fine. Fishhook traveled well.

Cousin Tom wrote his son at State College to tell him about all the plans. The next time Tom Junior came home, he brought a big footlocker with him. He had cleared out the closets at school and brought every experimental drug he could lay his hands on.

All the Iron Duff fox hunters joined in on the rejuvenation project. They began to feed Fishhook a special high-protein, high-bulk, low-fat, cholesterol-free diet. They gave him witch-hazel massages, end to end, three times a day. They gave him shots of hormones no one had ever even heard of.

Then they started on the vitamins: pills for all the ordinary-letter vitamins A through K, with double doses of vitamin E. A series of shots for all the B vitamins: B-12, B-13, B-14—all the way up to and including B-29. (They were determined to make a bomber out of him!)

Gradually, as this work went on, Fishhook was coming back to his old life. His appetite picked up; his disposition improved; his whole outlook about the future became more positive.

Pretty soon he was able to get up and walk around. Not long after that he began to show an interest when he heard the other dogs barking at night. By the time he got his B-29 shot, he was scratching at the door, begging to go out and chase foxes with the other dogs.

"No, Fishhook." Uncle Frank held him back. "You can't chase foxes, especially not on these dark nights. We've got too much invested in you. Besides, you have been restored for a higher calling."

Pretty soon old Fishhook seemed to be about as young as he was going to get, and the debate arose about which of the female dogs he should be mated with. All the Iron Duff fox hunters who had any kind of female dog at all quickly volunteered, but Uncle Frank held firm. His mind was made up. Old Belle was to be the one. He figured that with those long toenails she could keep her footing better, and Fishhook would have a better chance of being successful.

And so the great day arrived. Uncle Frank had kept Belle penned up for three days in a row so she would be all rested. He had a little fatherly talk with her about how they had restored Fishhook's body, but they weren't so sure about his memory—she might have to help him out with remembering a few things.

Old Belle and the new Fishhook were put in a little dog lot on the hill above Uncle Frank's house and left in privacy for the afternoon. Pretty soon the pleasant sounds rising into the air seemed to indicate that Fishhook's memory was at least as good as his body.

"I believe they know what they're doing," Tom told Uncle Frank.

Then all of a sudden a terrible sound was heard inside the dog lot: *yeeeooow!* Then—thump—something hit the ground.

Uncle Frank and the other assembled members of the Greater Iron Duff Fox Hunters' Association were almost afraid to open the gate. Still, the truth had to be faced.

Slowly they opened the gate to the dog lot and looked inside. There was Belle against the back fence. She was standing stock-still and seemed to be trembling a little. In the center of the lot, flat on his back on the ground, lay Fishhook, as Uncle Frank said later, "dead as a doornail."

They never knew what killed him, technically speaking. Dr. York came and looked him over, but he really couldn't tell anything. "Could have been a heart attack . . . could have been a stroke. It was pretty surely some kind of blowout." Beyond that speculation, no one knew.

It was sad when old Fishhook was buried. Not only was it sad to see him go, but there was also the great loss of hope that had been placed in his mating with Belle—hope, now gone, for a new bloodline in the Iron Duff foxhounds. Those were days of sadness.

A few weeks later, however, spirits soared. Suddenly it became evident that in that last great calling of his life, Fishhook had been effective. Belle was indeed going to have pups.

To hear Uncle Frank tell it, no woman in Iron Duff had ever been cared for the way that mother dog was spoiled during the ensuing weeks. She was confined to the barn and waited on hand and foot. As her time drew near, a special labor room was set up in one of the food rooms, and the members of the Greater Iron Duff Fox Hunters' Association signed on to sit with her in shifts around the clock.

On a cold, rainy night in March, just before four o'clock in the morning, Belle's pups were born. Except it wasn't "pups." It was just "pup." Out of all that hard work, out of all that expense, out of all that time and effort and hope, Belle had had just one pup.

But he was perfect. Beautifully shaped and marked, the little dog seemed to be a natural-born champion. Because of the night on which he was born, Uncle Frank named him Rainy Weather.

Rainy Weather was a prodigy of natural foxhound talent. Before he was old enough to stand and walk, he would roll his head around and sniff the air in a particular direction, and when Uncle Frank let the big dogs loose later, that would be exactly the direction in which they ran. Little Rainy Weather was smelling the fox scent, with all the doors and windows shut, before he was big enough to walk.

As the little dog grew up, the stories told about him were legion. People would say, "Rainy Weather? Why, that dog can smell with his nose taped up," and "Mr. Davis has got a dog can smell fox tracks underwater!" Everybody in Iron Duff was talking about Rainy Weather. And as he grew, he did indeed become a fabulous foxhound.

Of course, all the members of the Greater Iron Duff Fox Hunters' Association had very important thoughts on their minds. They knew that when Rainy Weather got to be 2 years old, they could send him up to New Jersey as the Iron Duff entrant in the National Foxhound Championship, and they were all sure he was a cinch to be Mister Foxhound U.S.A.

All the hunters did was watch him develop. There was no training to it. Rainy Weather knew by instinct exactly what to do before any suggestion could be offered by man or dog. It was just a matter of time until fame would be coming to Iron Duff. Uncle Frank and Cousin Tom began to get ready to take Rainy Weather to New Jersey.

A few arrangements had to be made before they could leave. Uncle Frank did, after all, milk and feed about 40 cows, and they all had to be milked and fed while he was gone. He usually had a dairyman on the farm to help out, but his dairyman had quit, and he hadn't hired a new one. He was going to have to hunt up some temporary help.

That was the problem. Most people in Iron Duff had about all the work they could keep up with, so the only people available for temporary employment were the subnatural Jolly boys.

Uncle Frank went up in the cove to Phyleete and Wife Jolly's house and hired their sons Lizard and Clogger. He brought them down to the dairy and took them into the feed room of the big barn to teach them what had to be done while he was gone.

It was slow going with Clogger because he literally took every step twice, but he was dependable. He was a great big overgrown boy and wore number-12 brogans on his feet. When those gunboat feet double-stepped into the feed room at the big barn, the old board floor just wouldn't hold, and Clogger stomped his way right through it.

"The ground's let me down again!" Clogger cried out.

"Aw, Clogger," Uncle Frank said, "that's not the ground. That's just the old rotten floor of the feed room. You stomped your way through the floor. Now you're standing on the ground. Look."

Uncle Frank began to pull the broken boards out of the way so that Lizard and Clogger could clearly see that Clogger was standing flat on the ground about six or eight inches below where the floor used to be.

Suddenly, even in the dim light of the feed room, they all saw the same thing at once. There in the dirt under the floor of the barn's feed room was a clearly visible set of fox tracks.

"Look, Mr. Davis," cried Lizard, "fox tracks! How did a fox get under the floor?"

Uncle Frank said, "The fox didn't get under the floor, boys. Why, that fox had to have come through here and left those tracks before this barn was ever built!"

"How long ago was that?" Lizard asked.

"Let's see . . . the barn has been here about 60 years. I remember Daddy building it when I was a little boy. Those tracks have to be at least that old, and I guess they could be a whole lot older."

"Go get Rainy Weather, Mr. Davis," Clogger begged.

"How come, Clogger?" Uncle Frank asked.

"See if he can foller that fox. Why, you know he can. Those tracks are clear as can be, and old Rainy Weather can foller tracks he can't even see at all!"

"Foxhounds follow by smell, Clogger. They don't have to see tracks, but they do have to smell them. And I can guarantee you that 60-year-old fox tracks . . . well, they may look good, but they surely don't have any smell left in them." Uncle Frank thought that ought to make some sense to the Jollys, but it didn't.

"Aw, let him try," begged Lizard. "Yeah, let him try," Clogger joined in. "It won't hurt to let him try!"

They wouldn't give up. They begged and annoyed Uncle Frank until he realized that nothing would convince the Jolly boys until they could see for themselves. He might as well let Rainy Weather have a useless and unfruitful sniff and get this over with.

While Uncle Frank went to get the dog, Lizard and Clogger cleared more of the boards away, and when Uncle Frank returned with Rainy Weather in tow, a good long set of fox tracks was visible. Suddenly Rainy Weather caught sight of those fox tracks. He yelped twice, jumped into the air, jerked loose from Uncle Frank, and, nose to the ground, took off after that fox that had passed through Iron Duff at least

60 years ago.

Getting started was the hard part. Rainy Weather jumped down through that hole that Clogger had stomped in the feed-room floor. He wiggled on his belly, following those tracks under that low-to-the-ground floor. When he came to the foundation of the barn, he dug his way under, then broke free into the feed lot, running and yelping for all he was worth.

"Look at him go, Mr. Davis!" Lizard exclaimed. He knew all the time that Rainy Weather could do it.

Uncle Frank stood open-mouthed and silent as Rainy Weather went out of the barnyard and right into a big cornfield, following the scent of a fox that had been long gone for well over half a century.

Rainy Weather was tearing that cornfield up. He was knocking corn down and throwing dirt every which way. "Why's he acting like that?" Lizard asked. "How come he don't just run up and down the rows?"

"Oh, Lizard," Uncle Frank answered, "that cornfield wasn't there 60 years ago. This was all woodland back then. Rainy Weather's just having to run around the trees like that fox did. Besides, boys, as many times as that field's been plowed during all the years since, he's having an awful time digging all those tracks back up and getting them in the right order!"

In a few minutes Rainy Weather had crossed the cornfield, broken out on the lower side, and started smelling and yelping his way across the lower-cove cow pasture. The dog would run straight for a while, jump sort of sideways in the air, then hit the ground and run some more. This odd jumping and running went on all across the cow pasture.

"How come he's jumping all around like that?" Clogger asked. "Ain't no reason for nobody to get that far above the ground."

"I've got that just figured out, Clogger," Uncle Frank assured him. "Years ago there was a fence row running right through where that pasture is now. Tore it out when I made the pasture bigger. Rainy Weather is having to jump over where that fence used to be every time that old fox jumped it. He's following the fox trail right through the air."

It was amazing. About then Rainy Weather came to a place where there had been a hole in the fence. The fox had without a doubt gone through that hole. Now, sniffing and following the trail, Rainy Weather tried to follow. Only trouble was that when the hole had been there, it hadn't been big enough for Rainy Weather to get through.

He hit the place where the hole had been and stuck right there in midair, wiggling and kicking. Everybody thought he was going to have to back up and go around, but he wiggled and kicked until he enlarged the place where the old hole had been and finally made it big enough that he could get through it.

After that Uncle Frank, Lizard, and Clogger got to worrying. They saw Rainy Weather running full speed with his nose to the ground, heading straight toward the flat field. Except the flat field wasn't there anymore. The flat field was where Uncle Frank had built the new pond. There Rainy Weather went, running and barking, straight toward the water.

That dog hit the edge of the pond and went straight to the bottom. On he went, out of sight, underwater, following the trail of that fox right across the bottom of the pond.

Of course, when Rainy Weather went under the water, they couldn't hear him barking. The quiet didn't last for long, though, because in a matter of seconds, bubbles began to come to the top of the water. Every time one of those bubbles popped, a little bark came out of it! The bubble-barks made a trail on top of the water, which marked Rainy Weather's progress across the bottom of the fishpond.

Rainy Weather's mother, Old Belle, had passed her long toenails along to her wonderful offspring. With those long toenails digging into the soft bottom of the pond, Rainy Weather was able to keep his speed up even underwater.

In fact, when he broke out of the water and was running on dry land again on the other side, he left the water so fast that he outran a whole bunch of bubbles. As they slowly rose to the top of the water and popped, it sounded for a brief time like two dogs barking at once: real barks and bubble-barks, back and forth, back and forth, until the bubbles ran out, and Rainy Weather was just barking on his own again.

Uncle Frank, Lizard, and Clogger stood there and listened while Rainy Weather barked his way up through Jolly Cove and out of sight over the ridge above the Greater Iron Duff Fox Hunters' Association headquarters.

Suddenly all the barking stopped. "What's happened to him?" Lizard asked. "He's stopped!"

"Oh, I don't think he's stopped," Uncle Frank answered. "You see, once he crossed that ridge above the fox-hunting house, he was on Sam Crawford's land. Sam's got a bunch of No Trespassing signs up over there, and Rainy Weather knows not to bark when he reads one of them. We'll hear him again in a little while."

Sure enough, it wasn't long until Rainy Weather started barking again. And so they listened to Rainy Weather bark, following the 60-year-old fox scent as he ran over the top of Kansada Mountain and faded from earshot.

A good foxhound will sometimes stay on a trail until he's completely exhausted. Some dogs just will not give up until they fall over on the ground, and still they struggle to bark, even when they can run no more. It was no surprise, then, when Rainy Weather had not come home at the end of the day.

Uncle Frank just figured he had run until his legs gave out, and the dog would come home in the morning, or some neighbor would spot him and call for Uncle Frank to come get him.

But the next day Rainy Weather did not come home. Up in the afternoon Uncle Frank got on the phone and called all the neighbors to see if anyone knew where he was. Several people had spotted him (or heard him and recognized his voice) heading west. Uncle Frank tracked Rainy Weather by telephone over into Jonathan's Creek, then Cataloochee, and finally on to Cosby, Tennessee, but there he lost him.

The next day he got into his truck and drove all around that part of the country, looking, talking to people, asking about signs of Rainy Weather. But the dog was nowhere to be found.

All the members of the Greater Iron Duff Fox Hunters' Association and many of their family members formed a search party. They divided up into a telephone committee, a dirt-road committee, a paved-road committee, a posted-land committee, and an Interstate 40 committee, all searching high and low for Rainy Weather. But he had simply vanished.

Uncle Frank and Tom had to cancel their trip to New Jersey. The National Foxhound Championship came and went, and for the first time in memory, no one representing Iron Duff was there.

Back in Iron Duff there was a time of mourning and great sadness among the fox hunters. The best dog they had ever known was gone, and that was that. Finally Uncle Frank suggested they all just put Rainy Weather out of their minds and get back to living in the present.

Days passed, then weeks. If Rainy Weather was not forgotten, he was at least no longer talked about. On the surface of things Iron Duff fox hunting returned to normal.

Nearly three months passed. Early one morning Uncle Frank was returning to the house after the morning feeding and milking. When he opened the kitchen door, the telephone was ringing.

He hurried to the phone, picked it up, and said hello to the early caller.

"Hello," replied a strange voice. "Is this Mr. Frank Davis?"

"Yes it is, in person," Uncle Frank answered.

"Do you live in some place called Iron Duff, North Carolina?"

"Yes, I do," Uncle Frank said. "Could you tell me who's calling?"

"This is the chief of police in Baltimore, Maryland," the voice replied.

"You don't say!" Uncle Frank had never talked to a big-city police chief before. "What can I do for you?"

"Well, Mr. Davis, I'm the one who may be able to do something for you. Let me see where to start . . . Mr. Davis, have you lost a dog?"

Lost a dog? Uncle Frank couldn't believe his ears. "Why, yes, I lost a dog . . . must have been three months ago . . . He was . . . "

The chief cut him off in mid-thought. "Listen, Mr. Davis, this morning we had a call about a break-in. It was down in a pretty tough part of town close to the inner harbor. Not much around there but pawn shops, beer joints, and secondhand stores."

"What's all this about?" Uncle Frank's patience was waning.

"Mr. Davis, somebody broke the front window out of a used-clothing store, set off the burglar alarm and everything. We sent two cars to the scene of the presumed crime. When they got there, they went inside to investigate. Nobody had touched the cash register; nobody had made a mess of anything; nobody had taken a thing. They couldn't figure it out."

Uncle Frank just listened.

"Then they heard a noise. Something was making an awful racket way back in the back of the store—that's the bargain department, where they keep all of the real worn-out stuff.

"They went back there, Mr. Davis, with their guns drawn, and when they got there, what they found was your dog, barking at an old worn-

218

out fox-fur coat! He was so hoarse you could hardly understand him."

Uncle Frank was silent with amazement.

"We got your address off his collar. Do you want him back?"

Uncle Frank had recovered his speech by now, and he answered, "Of course, I want him back. He's the finest dog I ever had. How do I go about getting him home again?"

"We've already checked that out," the chief replied. "The Trailways bus won't take him. We'll have to fly him back. That means we have to get an escort to take him to the airport, pay for what they call a sky kennel . . . Well, Mr. Davis, altogether it's going to cost over $200 to get your dog back."

"That sure is a lot of money," Uncle Frank seemed to think out loud. "How much is that fox-fur coat?"

"I don't know about that," the chief replied. "Let me ask the man who owns the place. I think he's still here at the station. Just hold on a minute."

Uncle Frank waited. The chief came back to the phone.

"The owner says that old coat could be 40, maybe 50 years old. Says he's bought and sold it a half-dozen times. He'll sell it to you for $10 plus postage just to get rid of it."

"Kathleen's been wanting a coat like that for a long time," was Uncle Frank's reply. "I'll tell you what. I can't afford to have the dog sent back, not for $200, but I'll send you the $10 if you'll send me that coat. Just do whatever you have to with that dog."

And so Rainy Weather was taken to the Baltimore dog pound, and that ancient, well-traveled, and well-worn fox-fur coat went in the U.S. mail, parcel post, to Aunt Kathleen.

About a week later Uncle Frank heard a noise coming down the road. It was the mailman's car, and about 20 yards behind, there was old Rainy Weather, nose to the ground, still barking with every step.

At the next meeting of the Greater Iron Duff Fox Hunters' Association, Rainy Weather was given a retirement party. It was decided that he didn't need to go to the National Foxhound Championship or anywhere else, for that matter, because he was already Mister Foxhound U.S.A.

Donald Davis grew up in a family of storytellers who have lived on the same Western North Carolina land since 1781. A former Methodist minister, now a performer and teacher, Davis has told his original stories to audiences since 1980. He lives in Ocracoke, North Carolina.

PERMISSIONS

Bruchac, Joseph. "Gluscabi and the Wind Eagle" from *Keepers of the Earth: Native American Stories and Environmental Activities for Children* by Michael J. Caduto and Joseph Bruchac, published by Fulcrum Publishing, 350 Indiana St. #350, Golden, Colo. 80401. Copyright © 1988 by Michael J. Caduto and Joseph Bruchac. Used by permission.

Clower, Jerry. "A Coon-Huntin' Story" from *Jerry Clower: Stories From Home,* published by the University Press of Mississippi. Copyright © 1992 by Jerry Clower. Used by permission.

Courlander, Harold. "Uncle Bouqui and Godfather Malice" from *Uncle Bouqui of Haiti*, published by Morrow Books. Copyright © 1942 by Harold Courlander. Used by permission.

Davis, Donald. "Rainy Weather" from *Barking at a Fox-Fur Coat*, published by August House. Copyright © 1991 by Donald Davis. Used by permission.

Forest, Heather. "The Tale of Dame Ragnel" from the recording *The Eye of the Beholder*, published by Yellow Moon Press. Copyright © 1990 by Heather Forest. Used by permission.

Hicks, Ray. "Jack and the Three Steers" from the recording *Ray Hicks Telling Four Traditional Jack Tales*, published by Folk-Legacy Records Inc. Copyright © 1964 by Folk-Legacy Records. Used by permission.

Hunter, Janie. "Barney McCabe" from the recording *Been in the Storm So Long*, published by Smithsonian/Folkways. Copyright © 1990 by Janie Hunter. Used by permission.

Lipman, Doug. "The Clever Wife of Vietnam" from the recording *Folktales of Strong Women*, published by Yellow Moon Press. Copyright © 1983 by Doug Lipman. Used by permission.

Martin, Rafe. "The Brave Little Parrot" from *The Hungry Tigress: Buddhist Legends and Jataka Tales*, published by Parallax Press. Copyright © 1990 by Rafe Martin. Used by permission.

O'Callahan, Jay. "The Herring Shed" from *Homespun: Tales From America's Favorite Storytellers*, published by Crown. Story copyright © 1988 by Jay O'Callahan. Used by permission.

Pennington, Lee. "The Calico Coffin" from *Homespun: Tales From America's Favorite Storytellers*, published by Crown. Story copyright © 1988 by Lee Pennington. Used by permission.

Reneaux, J. J. "Knock, Knock, Who's There?" from *Cajun Folktales*, published by August House. Copyright © 1992 by J. J. Reneaux. Used by permission.

Schram, Peninnah. "The Three Brothers" from *Jewish Stories One Generation Tells Another*, published by Jason Aronson. Copyright © 1987 by Jason Aronson Inc., Northvale, New Jersey. Used by permission.

Williamson, Duncan. "Mary and the Seal" from *Fireside Tales of the Traveller Children*, published by Canongate Publishing Ltd. Copyright © 1983 by Duncan Williamson. Used by permission.

INDEX OF STORIES

INDEX OF TELLERS